The Holidays
The Boys of Brighton

M. Tasia

ALSO BY M. TASIA

The Boys of Brighton series
Gabe
Sam's Soldiers
Rick's Bear
Jesse
Coop
Travis
Grady
Vincent
Shadow

EVERYONE LOVES THE BOYS OF BRIGHTON

"I loved this book and I love this town. I hope there's going to be more."
—Melissa Lemons on *Gabe*

"An amazing read that was filled with lust, love, crazy hot sex, danger, action and so much more This is the first book I have read in this series but I will definitely be reading more in the future."
—Gay Book Reviews on *Sam's Soldiers*

"I was crazy impressed that the author made me teary over the ending of a relationship that I shouldn't have even been invested in. I didn't yet know these characters yet the author made me hurt for them. That takes some mad writing skills!"
—Love Bytes Reviews

"Jesse and Royce together have my heart. Jesse has it all by himself."
—The Book Junkie Reads on *Jesse*

"So much action, intrigue, drama and angst for the long awaited story of Grady and Ben. This was worth the wait. Sexy and sweet. I can't wait for the next."
—SamD on *Grady*

"I knew this one would be my favorite to date! There was something about Vincent that said awesome then came Tristan."
—Booky on *Vincent*

"This installment of the Boys of Brighton was so good! I loved Shadow and Randy's story I was hooked from the first page to the last. This book was definitely worth the wait!"
—AG on *Shadow*

Welcome back to Brighton, Texas. Where any man can find home.

'Tis The Season

Some had waited years to find "the one," while others had given up on love and had closed themselves off from feeling anything. But each of these men have found the person that makes them whole, gives them hope and strength to face whatever life throws at them, and to show them what love really means. Welcome to the holidays in Brighton, Texas. Sit down and stay a spell. We invite you to soak up the joy of the season with your favorite lovers.

www.BOROUGHSPUBLISHINGGROUP.com

PUBLISHER'S NOTE: This is a work of fiction. Names, characters, places and incidents either are the product of the author's imagination or are used fictitiously. Any resemblance to actual events, locales, business establishments or persons, living or dead, is coincidental. Boroughs Publishing Group does not have any control over and does not assume responsibility for author or third-party websites, blogs or critiques or their content.

THE HOLIDAYS
Copyright © 2018 M. Tasia

All rights reserved. Unless specifically noted, no part of this publication may be reproduced, scanned, stored in a retrieval system or transmitted in any form or by any means, electronic, mechanical, photocopying, recording, or otherwise, known or hereinafter invented, without the express written permission of Boroughs Publishing Group. The scanning, uploading and distribution of this book via the Internet or by any other means without the permission of Boroughs Publishing Group is illegal and punishable by law. Participation in the piracy of copyrighted materials violates the author's rights.

ISBN 978-1-948029-53-7

ACKNOWLEDGMENTS

A HUGE Shout Out to Fans of the Boys of Brighton Series

It has been an honor bringing this world to life for all of you and I can't wait to take you on many more journeys through my upcoming series, Gates of Heaven, set in Downtown Los Angeles.

While writing this series, I've noticed that many of you have fallen in love with the town of Brighton itself. I completely understand. It became a character in its own right and I love it as well. In tribute of the tenth book in the Boys of Brighton Series, I've asked fans to tell me how they pictured Brighton. Some responded with how the town made them feel, others how they saw it as if they were there themselves, while others sent pictures. All found a connection to this town and these stories. Here are a couple of the many wonderful comments:

"I picture every building is different, borrowing this and that from another era. The buildings are an amazing jumble of different styles: rickety wooden shops, marble and brick houses, huge stone church, and the library would be the building that stands out the most. Winters are full of snow and summers are supper dry and hot." ~Kelly

"It's always sunny. People walking around, and kids playing in the park in the center of town. The Main Street stores are older, weathered white with different colored trim, and every store has a unique design but when you look at it from afar, it looks harmonious." ~Dagne

Thank you to each and every one of you for following along with me, and falling in love with the town and people of Brighton. Through the sorrow and forgiveness, trials and struggles, danger and intrigue, love and loss, you were there holding out for that happily-ever-after and I hope I've given it to you in spades.

AUTHOR'S NOTE

Thank you to every reader and fan out there. Without you, none of this would be possible. During the holiday season we tend to reflect on those things we are grateful for—family and friends, your pets, food on the table, and health, or simply making it through one more day. I'm thankful for those who give of themselves to help others. Those souls, like the people of Brighton, are priceless. I may have built a town out of my own desire to give everyone a safe place, but in reality, there are those among us who do that every day. For them, I am thankful.

From my family to you and yours, Happy Holidays.
xoxo Michelle

The Holidays

Brighton, Texas. Population 6,293 (and counting) – est. 1895

A town founded on the one guiding belief that families have the right to take any form, shape, or size. All are welcome and anyone can find their place here.

Chapter One

Gabe and Johnny

Johnny ran the tips of his scarred fingers across the raised lettering of his and Gabe's wedding invitation. The gold calligraphy seemed to dance across the page as his heart sped up at the thought that in less than thirty days he'd be marrying the man who'd literally saved his life, and then had shown him what real love felt like. The date was set for December twenty-fourth, Christmas Eve, and Johnny knew that no other present could ever compare to the vows they planned to say to one another.

The invitations had been sent out weeks ago, and now Johnny was busy creating a wedding scrapbook that they could show their children someday. Yes, that's right, children. Over a year ago they'd filled out copious amount of paperwork, had been visited by social workers a number of times, and then they were told to wait. Gabe and Johnny had been placed on an adoption waiting list, and it had been almost a year before they finally received word that a three-year-old girl from Costa Rica needed a loving home.

They'd been given the news two months ago. Gabe had been so excited that he'd called four times, texted eight times, and when he burst through the door of their home, Johnny would never forget Gabe's whooping and hollering when he tore down the hall and launched himself into Johnny's arms.

Lucy would be arriving in less than a week, and thanks to the help of the Mason clan—he loved those Masons—who worked by Gabe's and Johnny's sides, the guys believed they were ready. Well, as ready as anybody can be when a child was coming into their home.

On numerous occasions since they'd received the news, Johnny had been brought to tears at the thought of their daughter being with them on their wedding day. Of course, Lucy would be part of the event since they were a family. He wondered how overwhelmed she'd feel, but hoped by that time she'd know how much she was loved and wanted, and would see the wedding as a big party. Thankfully, the wedding had been planned down to the last napkin, so he and Gabe could spend their time with their daughter, making sure she felt she was home and loved.

The weather had cooled, with highs in the sixties and lows in the forties, but he was nice and warm. He'd set up a secondary office space in the corner of Gabe's greenhouse, among his love's stunning orchids. With his specially modified computer system, Johnny had been able to carry on after the fire damaged his hands and body. His clientele didn't care that he'd lost the full range of motion in a few of his fingers due to the nerve damage caused by the flames. As long as they received sound marketing advice and moneymaking advertisements, they were happy. However, with the pending arrival of their daughter, Johnny had scaled back his client roster so he could concentrate his time on Lucy.

Gabe would be home any minute from his shift at the fire station, the last one for a few months. He was taking parental leave so their family could bond. Since they'd begun submitting their paperwork, Gabe had been banking his leave time—no vacations this past year—to cover bonding leave when their child arrived.

Johnny heard Gabe's truck pull into their driveway and set his project aside for later; his man was home. Johnny pulled his jacket around himself and left the greenhouse. He went into the house through the patio doors and heard knocking on the front door. He was sure that had been Gabe's truck pulling up the drive, so why would he knock?

Johnny rushed to the door and opened it wide. What he found on the other side was a bit shocking. He was face-to-face with a bear. A stuffed bear almost the same size as he was with plush pink fur, big brown eyes, and a rainbow bowtie. He stepped back as the bear entered followed by his overjoyed fiancé.

"Honey, we have a lot of toys for Lucy already." Johnny didn't want to sound stern since Gabe's joy filled the room. There was no doubt who of the two of them would be the one spoiling their daughter.

"I couldn't say no to Ms. Snuffle Van Bearstein when I saw her in the window over at Marie's toy shop."

"Who?" Johnny asked. Gabe held out a framed birth certificate with gold and pink curlicues around the edges. Sure enough, Ms. Van Bearstein's name was on it. "Well, as long as it's all legal, I guess it's okay," Johnny joked as he took Gabe's duffle bag and set it on the couch. The sight of Johnny's large, muscled firefighter holding a giant pink teddy bear made him melt. The strong, dominant man who thrived on control and taking care of others was completely blown away, and undone, by their daughter's impending arrival.

Years ago, Gabe had pulled Johnny out of a burning building, sat with him for days on end in the hospital, and then brought him home, opening his world to unconditional love. He could imagine what his loving man would do for his child.

Gabe set the new bear on the chair and pulled Johnny into his arms. "I love you, Johnny."

He couldn't help but sink into Gabe's arms; the man was irresistible. "I love you too, honey. Should we go find a home for the new arrival?"

"Definitely." Gabe smiled. "But first, I've been dreaming of doing this all day." Johnny was swept up into Gabe's arms, and turned until his back was pressed against the living room wall.

Gabe didn't give Johnny a chance to catch his breath. He was being kissed by a man enflamed. Gabe thoroughly mapped Johnny's mouth with an eager tongue before releasing him, leaving him hard and needy. Johnny held on to his fiancé's hand for a few seconds. He needed to allow his head to stop spinning while adjusting his jeans. Gabe had a way of taking over, leaving Johnny dizzy from the onslaught, but he wouldn't have it any other way.

Once he regained the ability to walk, Johnny followed Gabe down the hallway with Lucy's big pink bear in tow. As soon as they got the news, they'd rushed out and bought paint and furniture to convert one of the guestrooms into their daughter's bedroom. Johnny had designed the room to be airy and calm by suggesting they paint it a soft muted blue with an occasional cloud or bird in the sky. Gabe had painted the blue and Johnny painted the clouds, birds, and tree on the far side of the longest wall. A small play table sat under the painted leaves, and Lucy's hand-crafted wooden bed, sat a few feet away. A gift from Gabe's aunts, who knew many local artists through their shop, Hidden Treasures. They'd had the bed commissioned.

The closet was full of clothing in their daughter's size and bigger. The adoption agency had provided Lucy's measurements as well as a few precious photographs. The child's toy box was filled to the brim as Gabe proudly set Ms. Van Bearstein in the center of the white duvet covering the bed.

"Perfect," Gabe announced with pride before pulling Johnny close. "Absolutely perfect."

Johnny knew he wasn't only commenting about the room. It had been a hard road getting to this place, but now that they'd arrived at this point, Johnny could be philosophical about what they'd been through. The fire had brought him Gabe, and the time he'd spent healing gave them time to get to know one another, to explore their deep feelings, wants, and desires. The physical trauma of losing the full use of his hands had taught Johnny patience while he worked through physiotherapy. And while he would have been all too happy not to have experienced the pain knowing this about himself, Chris, Gabe's ex, had taught Johnny to fight for what he wanted.

His life had completely changed compared to when he lived under his father's rule. He hadn't heard from his father in over three years, which was odd, given his father thrived on controlling his sons.

That thought reminded him. "Frank sent me another email today. He received the invitation to our wedding." His brother still lived in the same Manhattan condominium for the past eight years, making it easy to track him down.

"What did your brother have to say?" Gabe asked, unable to conceal his concern.

Johnny understood the trepidation. He and Frank had lost touch for what felt like a lifetime. Johnny had assumed his brother had been living the life of a celebrity plastic surgeon and had no time for him. About the same time his father had thankfully decided to lose interest in Johnny, unfortunately, so did Frank. Which made sense since the communication stopped a little before his brother and father became partners in their own practice.

"That he may be able to come to our wedding." Even though they'd lost touch, Johnny still wanted his brother there when he married Gabe.

"Really?" Gabe sounded shocked.

"Yes. What do you think?" Johnny asked, because at the moment he didn't even have a clue as to how he felt about it. He'd asked figuring he'd receive no response or a no. The "maybe" yes had surprised him.

"Honestly, that he wants something," Gabe stated bluntly.

"Why? I don't have anything."

"You haven't talked to your brother in years and then suddenly he's free for our wedding. It's suspicious." Gabe shook his head.

Johnny couldn't disagree. The sudden "warming" was odd. Now that Gabe knew Frank might come to the wedding, he'd be in protection mode if Frank showed, which meant he'd be keeping an eye on the man.

"I know it's out of character for him to say yes, and we talked about me sending the invitation, but I need to know why he stepped out of my life like that."

"You may not like the answer, baby." Gabe held him close. "But I'll be right by your side."

Johnny never doubted that for a second.

***

Five days later Gabe was sitting next to Johnny in one of the adoption agency's offices, which they had decorated to look more like a living room. They were waiting for their daughter to arrive. Gabe was excited and terrified at the same time, but he had to be strong for Johnny, who looked two seconds away from an emotional breakdown. His love had such a soft and caring heart, Gabe knew he was lucky to have him, and little Lucy was about to learn how special a daddy Johnny would be.

"What if she's afraid of us?" Johnny asked, squeezing Gabe's hand tight.

"This is all new to her, baby. She's bound to be afraid of a lot of things until she becomes accustomed to our home and to us." Gabe went with logic to try to calm his fiancé.

"What if I screw up?"

"All new parents feel that way."

"If we have to wait much longer, I think I might pass out," Johnny admitted. Gabe was unsure if he was joking or not, so he pulled his chair closer in case.

Gabe had been dreaming of this moment for many years and it was finally here. He was finally getting the family he'd dreamed of, and he couldn't be happier. Of course, he and Johnny were a family already but with so much love to give, it made sense to share it. Providing a child with a safe, loving home where they could grow in peace was natural to him.

He thought he'd try to take Johnny's mind off the waiting. "Jesse called to say Randy finished the mural in Haven so everything is moving as planned and should be ready for the wedding and reception."

Jesse and Royce were almost at the end of construction on the new Safe Haven Center for the LGBTQ+ community's teenagers and adults in crisis. Everyone called it Haven for short. It combined housing, schooling, and counseling for anyone in need. Many of the homeless youths were escaping violence, and/or were kicked out of their family homes because of their sexual orientation or gender identity. The Haven was open to anyone who needed a safe place until they could get back on their feet.

Gabe and Johnny had decided to have their wedding there on Christmas Eve in celebration of new beginnings. For them, for Haven, and for all the people who would be helped in the coming years.

Before Johnny could respond to Gabe's comment, the door to the room opened and Mrs. Connor, the representative from the adoption agency, walked in carrying an adorable toddler in her arms. Lucy Rose Mason. Her brown hair was up in a ponytail, her beautiful dark eyes looked around the room, and her chubby cheeks showcased the cutest dimples.

Their daughter Lucy was perfect.

They both stood, unsure if they should approach her or wait for her to come to them. Thankfully, Mrs. Connor took that decision out of their hands.

"Why don't the two of you sit down in the play area and we'll join you," she suggested.

"Thank you," Gabe said in relief.

"It's normal for parents to be cautious, not wanting the first time they meet their child to be stressful. I've seen children leave here in tears and others in laughter. Neither reaction has any effect on the bond that will grow weeks and months into the future. Please don't worry."

Gabe led Johnny to the thick rug in the play area and they sat cross-legged on the floor. Mrs. Connor brought Lucy over; her tiny head was turning left and right trying to see everything in the room. Gabe's heart was racing as his daughter was placed on the floor, among the toys, a foot away from them.

At first, she looked a bit unsure until Johnny got down on his belly and began playing with the toys. Leave it to him to break the ice. Lucy joined right in as if she'd done this a thousand times. Gabe lay down on the other side of their daughter, picked up a plush stuffed puppy, and began to play with it. The three of them carried on like this, playing with and talking to Lucy, who seemed to accept their presence.

"I see the scar from her surgery is healing well," Johnny whispered to Mrs. Connor.

Gabe had noticed the scar on his daughter's top lip. Lucy had had surgery to repair her cleft lip and palate.

"Yes, the surgeon with Doctors Without Borders has helped children from the orphanage before and, apparently, is well known in his field. He did an amazing job and her speech has improved because of it," Mrs. Connor explained.

"How delayed is her speech?" Gabe asked.

"I was told six months. On occasion she will repeat a small word but hasn't managed to put two words together quite yet."

Gabe's heart skipped a beat when Lucy crawled over to him and handed Gabe a block before taking the stuffed puppy he was holding. His cheeks hurt, he was smiling so wide. "Do you like the puppy, Lucy? He's soft, isn't he?" She probably had no idea what he was saying, but her toothy smile was all the response he needed.

"Pu...pup," Lucy said as she bounced the stuffed animal on the ground.

"Yes, puppy. You have a puppy," Johnny's voice cracked slightly as he spoke, his emotions riding close to the surface.

Gabe knew those were happy tears gathering in those stunning green eyes, but apparently Lucy didn't. She scooted herself closer to

Johnny before handing him the puppy. In all honesty, she sort of mushed it into Johnny's face, but it produced the same result. Johnny held the stuffed puppy as if it were the most precious gift he'd ever received.

That was how their new family began their life together.

Years later, when their daughter would surely ask why a raggedy stuffed puppy was tucked away in the safe, Gabe would explain how it was her Pop's most prized possession.

Chapter Two

Sam, Dante, and Spider

Dante backed the final trailer up to the garage of a colorful bungalow located pretty much in the center of Brighton. An American flag attached to the front porch blew in the wind of the cool December afternoon, but Dante couldn't have felt warmer or happier than he was at this moment. Sam, the man responsible for this day, walked out the front door and up to the rear of the trailer. Other team members had already returned to the main house in their compound to get things ready for the barbeque celebration.

He shut the truck off and stepped out onto the newly mowed lawn, which they had cut yesterday when they had gotten back from another mission. The house hadn't been lived in for a little while and would need to have a few things repaired and refreshed, but his mom had loved it the first time she'd laid her eyes on it.

Yes, Joanne and Frank Phillips had moved to Brighton, and Dante was ecstatic along with his partners Sam and Spider. Truthfully, if it hadn't been for Sam's digging, and his huge, unrelenting heart, none of this would be happening. Dante tried not to think of the many years wasted due to a stupid misunderstanding, and while he wished he could get them back, he knew he couldn't undo the past. Now, he had a chance to rebuild his relationship with his foster parents, who had been "real" parents, and it was full steam ahead.

"Are you going to help with these boxes or are you going to stand there all day looking at the lawn?" Sam asked while juggling two boxes in his arms.

"Yes, Trouble, I'm coming," Dante huffed good-naturedly, receiving a glowing smile from his fiery redheaded lover before he walked back into the house.

A lot had happened since he and Spider first met Sam. Between houses blowing up, and adding Randy, Shadow's partner, the latest member to the Sentinel's ranks of significant others, it had been a nonstop several months. However, now they were taking some time off, the whole team, to enjoy the holidays, and the New Year with the people they loved.

Spider came out the open garage door and he immediately wrapped his arms around Dante. "Happy, love?"

"Yes, and I'll be much happier when we get this couch in the house," Dante grumbled before nibbling the side of Spider's thick neck. "Then I can get you and Sam home and start the real fun."

"That's sounds perfect," Spider moaned as Dante continued to explore.

"Sounds good to me too," Sam laughed as he popped up in between them exactly where they liked him. Spider kissed the side of Sam's head while Dante mapped his mouth with his tongue. His men meant the world to him, and the love the three of them shared was forever growing.

"You three can't help yourselves, can you?" his mom asked from somewhere behind them. His parents supported the fact that they'd become a triad, and seemed to fit in well with the Brighton philosophy of accepting families of all shapes and sizes.

"Spider's the one who started it," Dante threw his love right under the bus—figuratively.

"You little shit," Spider growled before laughing along with Sam and his parents.

The three broke up their impromptu love-fest of sorts and attacked the rest of the boxes and furniture. Once they had everything placed where his mom wanted it, for the fourth or fifth time, the four men collapsed onto the couch they'd just moved...again. Dad took a drink from his water bottle before calling an end to the day's activities.

"Joanne, sweetheart, stop before I gain a hernia along with this money pit," Dad joked as he stretched out his back. "I'm getting too old for this."

"First, it's a beautiful house, and second, you were told not to lift anything heavy by the entire team, your son, Spider, and Sam. So don't be whining about it now."

Leave it to Mom to cut straight through the bullshit. It was her gift. Dante couldn't help but laugh. He'd missed this. Hell, he'd missed everything about the two people who had saved his life. Without Frank and Joanne Phillips, Dante seriously doubted whether he'd be alive today. When he was young, after his father had taken off and his mother drank herself to death, he was left in the care of his sadistic uncle. After one beating, he'd gone to the Phillipses' house for help after not being able to stop his nosebleed by himself. He never returned to his uncle's "care."

Sometimes, Dante questioned his good fortune after finding Spider. Then the two of them found Sam, and now having his parents back in his life it all seemed too good to be true. It was overwhelming and exhilarating at the same time.

This year he'd be counting his blessings with his family.

***

Spider drove their truck back to their big old Victorian. On the way, they stopped to admire the holiday decorations making their appearance all over town. It seemed everywhere you looked there were menorahs or Kwanza baskets in windows, tinkling multicolored lights, flowers, tinsel, ribbon, and sparkling bulbs hanging from trees and bushes. He hadn't had the chance to enjoy a real Christmas in a long time. Of course, he, Dante, and their team had celebrated one way or another, but they'd usually been on missions at the time.

This year they'd be home with their loved ones without having to dodge any incoming rounds, or burrow in some hellhole tunnel.

The Sentinels' house had been decorated with the help of the entire team and their partners. At night, it shone like a beacon with all the lights they had strung up on it. The one time he'd mentioned that they might have overdone it, he was banished to the garage to untangle four more boxes of the twinkling bastards. Spider never made that mistake again.

Both Dante and Sam were lost in thought, but both had smiles on their faces, which made Spider happy. His parents had died a long time ago, while he was still in the military, but between the Masons and Dante's parents, and their team family, Spider never felt lonely.

Of course, he missed his folks, but the pain was a bit lighter having all the people he cared about and who cared about him around.

As they pulled up to the house, all that cheery goodness was out on display for Dante's parents' arrival. Their car pulled up right behind Spider's truck and everyone jumped out. The wind blew colder as night had fallen, but at least he wasn't shoveling snow. There were benefits to this milder weather they were having.

"Sons, it's beautiful," Joanne's voice cracked, and Sam wrapped his arms around her as Frank stood between Dante and Spider. Sam's heart knew no bounds, and all Spider could say was that he was blessed to have his love.

"You've done good, boys," Frank said as he placed his arms over their shoulders and gave them a hug. "We're so proud to be a part of your family."

Dante and Spider hugged him back and the five of them walked up the blinking walkway into the shiny house. Once they opened the doors, two excited dogs and a pack of puppies greeted them with licks and barks. Buddy was wearing reindeer antlers and Luna had on a candy cane collar while their puppies, all six of them, had miniature collars with Christmas colors on display.

"It's like Christmas blew up in here." Spider could hear the disbelief in his own voice.

The team had been busy while the five of them finished off the Phillipses's new house. Garland was strung across the wide living room from all points on the ceiling. The furniture was covered in themed pillows, and the tables were covered with beautiful red and green linens. Several sconces now had themed light bulbs, and everywhere he looked, stars, Christmas trees, angels, reindeer, and snowmen covered every flat surface in the house. The big Christmas tree they'd set up a few days ago was now covered with even more lights, and a large fluffy white tree skirt was wrapped around its base with wrapped presents loaded beneath it.

"How long have we been gone?" Dante asked, sounding as shocked as he felt.

"This team rocks," Sam cheered as he ran around looking at the decorations and checking out the tags on each of the presents.

A heavenly smell was coming from the back of the house, so they followed their noses to the screened-in back patio. There were space heaters to assure everyone stayed warm while the barbeques flamed away at the far end. Once they stepped over the threshold, the team cheered, raising their drinks in celebration.

"It isn't Christmas yet?" Dante asked as he held on to Spider's and Sam's hands.

"We don't need an occasion to celebrate being together, we're a family," Shannon explained before she wrapped her arm around Jackson Bowen. They'd been dating since meeting on their last mission to protect Randy from Jackson's brother.

Spider could feel the slight tremble in Dante's hand before he spoke. "I want to thank all of you, every single one. I…I remember the child I was, wishing for this, and you've all given that to me. It's a gift I can never repay."

Both he and Sam were quick to gather Dante into their arms. Their triad and their extended family could never be replaced. He looked out to see every member of his team, with their partners, along with Frank and Joanne, holding a glass up. Matthew quickly brought over three glasses of beer for them.

Dante raised his glass and shouted, "To family."

"To family," everyone cheered in unison with a few barks from the puppies added in to round out the joy.

It wasn't fancy, there was no champagne, and there were more than a few ripped jeans in the group, but he couldn't have been in finer company.

It was his and it was perfect.

***

Sam set the last plate into the dishwasher, closed the door, and turned it on. He didn't want to leave a mess for Mrs. Walker. Frank and Joanne had gone home, a few of the team members were still hanging out in the living room while others had already said their good nights and were off to bed. Spider walked into the kitchen with the lasts bits of trash, deposited them in the garbage, and took Sam into his arms.

He loved the feeling of being in his lovers' tattooed, muscled arms. His men were gods and he was a lucky and happy man. They loved him so completely that Sam never had any doubts since they'd sorted out their bumps in the road to forever.

"Are Dante's parents okay with going to Gabe and Johnny's wedding?" They were new to town and told Sam they didn't want to impose even though Johnny had invited them.

"Yeah, they're good once we explained that most of the town would be there at some point during the day," Spider assured as he nibbled down the side of Sam's neck. "I've sent Dante to have a shower, baby. Do you want to go and help scrub his back?" Spider asked before lifting Sam off the floor and into his arms. "I'll scrub yours."

Sam couldn't help the small moan that escaped as Spider kissed and nuzzled the side of his neck. He basked in the attention Spider was giving him. The three of them had fought tooth and nail for their happy ending, and he'd never take any of this for granted.

He could feel they were moving down the hallway toward their suite of rooms, but chose to concentrate on Spider's glorious lips instead. Spider's teeth scraped against his sensitive skin, causing goosebumps to rise all over his overheated body.

As soon as they closed the door to their private realm, they began stripping at a frantic pace, desperate to get back in each other's arms. The second his boxers hit the floor, Sam jumped up into his lover's waiting embrace and dove in for a deep kiss full of tongues and teeth. He could hear the water running in their walk-in shower and Spider turned in that direction.

Sam knew Dante would already know they were there. No one could sneak up on the man. Spider carried Sam straight into the shower and into Dante's open arms.

"There you are, beautiful. I've been waiting for my men to join me," Dante said in a way that felt like he was claiming them all over again.

Sam felt Spider cover his back and he found himself back in his favorite place, cuddled between his men. The brilliantly colored tattoos on his arms stood in contrast to Dante and Spider's black and gray military designs. He loved that about himself and his men, the differences, which only made them a stronger triad.

His men's hands ghosted across his sensitive skin as they explored his body while Sam chased the beads of water running down Dante's neck with his tongue.

"God I love the two of you so much," Dante growled, taking Spider's lips in a demanding kiss before turning and doing the same to Sam.

Once he could breathe again Sam replied, "I love you too, Dante." Then turning his head he looked Spider in the eyes. "I love you, Jack. I don't know how I ever lived without the two of you."

"You'll never have to find that out, baby. I love you and Dante, and plan to spend the rest of my life like this," Spider explained before he reached for the waterproof lube they kept in the shower. "Now, I need to be balls deep inside you."

Soon Sam felt Spider's thick finger circling his hole, loosening the tight muscles. Then a second finger joined it from the opposite side. Dante. His two lovers worked together until Sam was a writhing mess whimpering between them. His hard cock felt like it was ready to explode, but he fought off his orgasm with everything he had, this wasn't ending so soon.

Spider took him into his arms and pressed his back against the cool tile wall. Sam wrapped his legs around his lover's muscled waist and began sucking marks up on his neck, Sam's cock finding much needed friction against Spider's rippled abdomen.

"Hold on, baby, no coming yet," Spider groaned loudly, and Sam felt the large, spongy head of Spider's cock at his entrance.

"I need—" Whatever he was about to say was cut off by his own deep moan as Spider sank his thick cock deep in one slow stroke.

Sam felt full as every nerve ending in his body screamed to life while he held on to his lover's shoulders and watched as Dante approached Spider from behind. Spider's body shook as he waited for Dante to prepare him for his cock. Sam couldn't hold still no matter how hard he tried and began pushing himself farther down on Spider's throbbing shaft.

"Dante, sweetheart. You'd better make this quick. I need you inside me before Sam has me pounding him into the tile."

Dante must have taken Spider at his word because in under a minute Dante was stepping up behind Spider to slide himself in. Spider moaned in Sam's ear, every hitch in Spider's breath and tremble in his body sent Sam further into a world of pure pleasure.

Spider moved Sam up and down on his cock while Sam took the opportunity to rub his needy shaft against Spider's abs. Dante hissed as he pulled out of Spider and slammed right back in, causing Sam to slide even farther down on Spider's cock. All three moaned as their triad joined, and soon the sound of skin meeting skin and men groaning filled their en suite.

Dante leaned forward and took Sam's lips in a demanding kiss as he pounded into Spider while Spider did the same to Sam. He ran his hands over both of his men. Their pupils were blown wide open as both of his lovers looked at Sam with raw, passionate love. That was Sam's tipping point, without one more rub against Spider's tight abs, Sam came in long, pulsing streams against Spider.

He felt Spider's cock pulse as Sam's own muscles squeezed his lover tight until he too came with a loud roar. Sam's eyes were fuzzy as he watched Dante's face transformed from almost pain and need into unadulterated joy and pleasure. It was beautiful to witness his men at their most vulnerable.

Dante leaned his head on Spider's back as Sam leaned back against the now warm tile wall. Spider stood supporting both of them without a single complaint. Sam felt his men washing his body and heard their murmuring voices, but all the day's activity had caught up with him, and all he could do was enjoy the ride.

The next thing he knew he was dried and cuddled in the middle of the bed as Dante and Spider turned off the lights. His lovers climbed into bed on either side of him, each wrapping one of their arms over him, loving and protecting him, as was their nature.

"You know I think there's a saying somewhere that you never really meet the ones you were meant to love, because a part of them has been with you all along." Sam spoke just above a whisper. "A part of each of you has been with me from the beginning. I like the sound of that."

Dante leaned over and softly kissed Sam. "I like the sound of that too, beautiful."

Spider kissed his way up from Sam's shoulder until he took control of his lips. Once they parted he said, "When we met, it felt like a part of me recognized you the same way it recognized Dante when we first met."

Sam looked up at his men. "This is exactly where I want to be. No doubts, no regrets, only love."

Dante and Spider looked at each other then back down at Sam. Every emotion was plain to see on their faces: joy, desire, contentment, awe, and profound love.

There wasn't really a need for more words, was there?

Chapter Three

Rick, Bear, and Josh

Rick gathered up the parade of action figures, dolls, blocks, and books from the living room floor for the second time today, knowing he'd be doing it all over again soon enough. The thought brought a smile to his face. He would have never believed it if someone had told him sixteen months ago that he'd be clearing a path through his nephew's toys so his partner could bring in boxes of Christmas decorations from the garage.

Josh was down for his afternoon nap after his play date with Lucy, Gabe and Johnny's newly adopted daughter. The toddler was such a joy, and the pride Rick saw on her parents' faces was unmistakable. Lucy was adjusting well, but didn't wander far away from her dads too often quite yet. She would only allow Johnny and Gabe to lift and carry her, which was completely understandable. After all, everything was all new to her, including the language.

But the one thing she seemed to understand was that she was loved.

This quiet time while Josh was napping would give Rick and Bear the chance to set up the tree by the bay window in their living room. As he went along, Rick couldn't help but look at the pictures that now covered the walls. Front and center was a large picture of Jenny, Josh's mother and Bear's sister, the same dark blue eyes as her brother seemed to watch him as he cleaned. Their new family had done so much since Jenny's death it was sometimes hard to believe that Rick, the anxiety-ridden librarian, was a part of his own family now—toddler included.

Most of the photographs strewn around the house he'd taken. Trips to Dallas and South Padre Island, Kemah Boardwalk, the Children's Museum in Houston, and even a two-day getaway for him and Bear in Galveston Beach were displayed in a variety of frames. Josh had been in the loving care of the White Hair Crew while they were gone. After all, they were the mothers to the whole town.

His life had changed so significantly. It wasn't that his anxiety had magically disappeared, but due to the amazing man who was carrying two boxes through the doorway, Rick had found a way to enjoy life one day at a time.

He jumped out of the way as Bear set the boxes down. The larger of the two contained their big, bushy artificial tree. After hearing the stats on how many fires live trees caused, there was no way he was bringing one into their house. *An average of two hundred structural fires annually in the U.S. caused by Christmas trees.* Now Rick couldn't help but smile at his info-drop, when before Bear, Rick would have chastised himself for his idiosyncrasies. Bear had helped Rick accept that it was part of him and not to feel ashamed when he did it in front of people. Rick was still working on that.

The tree they'd purchased last year before Jenny's death looked like a Virginia pine so there wasn't really a difference if it was alive or not in Rick's mind. Besides, they had a few trees decorated and lit in their yard if anyone wanted to see a living tree sparkle and shine.

Bear turned to Rick and wrapped him in his big arms. "Excited, baby?"

"Yep. You know I love Christmas." Rick had been passionate about Christmas for as long as he could remember. "I enjoy the closeness everyone feels toward each other, the love they share and gifts they give. It's perfect."

"And so are you," Bear softly growled before taking Rick's lips in a deep, exploring kiss. Though Rick wasn't so sure about that, his boyfriend was convinced and stated it often.

It was always a boost knowing that Bear saw him that way. No one else had ever suggested anything even close to perfect in the same sentence as Rick Johansson. It had taken him a while to accept that, but he no longer argued when his lover said it.

"I have three more boxes in the garage plus all the new decorations you've been ordering over the last year." Bear rolled his eyes in mock exasperation.

"Isn't it amazing? You can buy Christmas stuff all year long," Rick gushed, as if that was Christmas magic all by itself.

"I don't know about amazing but I do know it's heavy. Are you sure there isn't too much?" Bear asked for what had to be the tenth time.

"You said the same thing about Easter, July Fourth, and Thanksgiving, but didn't they turn out to be amazing holidays?"

"Yeah, they did," Bear agreed before pulling Rick close and nuzzling the side of his head with a wild beard that tickled. He loved that his big, burly biker was unafraid to show his love. "You've outdone yourself every time. I'm positive that everything you put into it helped Josh through it without his mother. I know it helped me cope without Jenny. You are an incredible man. I love you beyond what I ever thought was possible."

Rick had wanted to make the holidays easier on his family and was happy to hear that it had worked. It had been a year of ups and downs, both emotionally and physically, but they'd survived and flourished together. Rick ran his hand over the scars on his abdomen left by a piece of the engine, which had impaled him after he'd run the car he'd been forced to drive by Josh's attempted kidnapper off the road.

"I love you too, Bear. I love Josh, and I love our new life together. I wouldn't change it for the world," Rick said before giving his love a quick kiss and then a slap to his muscled ass. "Now back to work. My master plan requires time to assemble."

Bear laughed softly, trying not to wake Josh before releasing Rick and heading back to the garage for another load. Rick turned and dug into the first box, his mind awhirl with decor ideas. He pulled out strand after strand of colorful lights, as well as garland and ribbon. He'd always liked colored Christmas lights because it had been his mother's favorite. Carefully he set his mom's nativity scene aside. He would construct the tableau with porcelain figurines on the fireplace mantel to keep it safe. He would never leave Josh out of the fun of putting everything together, so the painted, wooden nativity scene would be assembled lower within Josh's reach.

Smaller boxes containing the different bulbs were placed on the end of their large sectional couch until they put up the tree. Everything was moving along quickly as he emptied box after box of Christmas decorations until the living room was full. He couldn't imagine being happier than he was at that moment.

"Rick, baby, why don't you come sit down on the couch with me for a moment," Bear asked, and Rick turned to find his man sitting in his usual spot in the corner of the sectional. He always said the corner was his because he could hold Rick and Josh on either side of him.

Rick set the tinsel down and walked over to his lover, who had a package wrapped in brown shipping paper on his lap. When they were first getting to know each other, Bear would bring Rick first editions from his favorite author, Tom Clancy. The memory brought a huge smile to his face. The little things his man would do for him only reinforced the rock-solid love they shared.

"What's this?" Rick asked as he cuddled into Bear's waiting arms.

"It's a surprise," Bear replied before biting his lip. "I wanted to give you this not as a Christmas gift but as something from me to the man I love."

Rick hugged Bear close before taking the package in his hands. He opened it, careful not to damage anything beneath the paper. Sure enough, there was a book under the wrapping but it wasn't a novel but a hardcover picture book. Rick looked up at Bear, who only smiled in return.

He opened the first page and found a picture of the four of them, Rick, Bear, Josh, and Jenny before she was hospitalized. The next was a picture of him asleep on Bear's chest, and then one of him sitting at Josh's bedside reading him a book, playing in the backyard in their new sandbox. The next was Josh asleep in Rick's arms as they lay on the couch, and another of Rick covered in sticky marshmallow the day they decided to make s'mores.

The pictures went on and on until Rick came to the end and found a small velvet bag attached to the binding. He looked up at Bear once again.

"Open it, sweetheart," Bear whispered.

Rick could feel his heart racing as he undid the knot with his shaky fingers and reached inside. The metal was warm against his skin and Rick couldn't stop the tears from falling while he removed the gold band from the bag. There were three square-cut diamonds set in the band and engraved on the inside the words *"Simply Perfect."*

***

Bear could feel his heart doing a drum solo in his chest. He hoped it was excitement and not that he might be having a heart attack.

Rick twisted around until he was facing him. "Bear, it's beautiful."

"Not nearly as much as you are to me," Bear admitted honestly. "The book are pictures of you when you weren't looking. I wanted to show you what I see when I look at you. The love, the bravery, the beauty that is all you, Rick, and I'm the lucky one to have you. I never dreamed I'd have this life, never thought it was possible for me. Who'd think an enforcer with an MC out of Chicago would be given this chance. And I can tell ya, I'm not going to blow it. Marry me, baby. Make an honest man out of me."

Bear brushed the tears off his love's red cheeks. He knew Rick was having a hard time getting himself together, but was surprised when he shoved the ring into Bear's hands. However, at the same moment, Rick extended his left hand and he knew what his love wanted. Bear decided to go all the way. He carried Rick to the center of the living room, surrounded by toys, boxes, and Christmas decorations, and Bear dropped to one knee in front of the man he loved.

"Rick, will you marry me?" Words Bear never thought would come from his mouth now flowed freely to the man who'd changed his world so completely. "Make me the luckiest man on this planet."

"Y-yes. I...I love you, Bear," Rick answered as his voice cracked with emotion.

Bear slid the band onto the third finger of Rick's left hand and then kissed it to seal the deal. Rick clung to him and slid down onto the ground and into Bear's lap. Though Rick was still in tears, Bear knew they were happy tears and shed a few of his own.

There they sat, in each other's arms in a sea of tinsel. It was exactly how Bear wanted it. Real life, not some make-believe moment achieved by spending exorbitant amounts of money. He wasn't saying Rick wasn't worth that, because he was, but that wasn't them. This was real, right here.

"We'll pick a date once the holidays and Gabe and Johnny's wedding are over. I know it will be hard to keep it small, being in

Brighton and all, but maybe we could have the ceremony outside." Rick was making plans and Bear's heart sang.

"You can plan it any way you want it, baby. I'm sure the White Hair Crew would love to help us."

"I bet they would. That would be great," Rick near shouted with excitement. Bear had to shake himself that he was the one giving Rick this. Bear was the cause of Rick's happiness and intended to keep doing it until Bear breathed his last breath. "We should get back to it. We should at least have the tree up for Josh to help decorate when he wakes up."

"He will be the ring bearer, and maybe Lucy would like to be the flower girl….wait, stop. One thing at a time, Christmas first, right." Bear couldn't help but be excited. It wasn't like him to run ahead of himself, but hell, he was marrying Rick. "You're my fiancé now."

"Fiancé," Rick whispered before breaking out into one of his full-on beautiful smiles. "You're my fiancé too."

"I can tell you honestly, I never thought I'd have one," Bear said in awe. "Never thought I'd be this lucky."

"Same here," Rick agreed, never once losing his smile.

Bear stood and helped Rick to his feet. While Rick continued emptying boxes, Bear got busy setting up the tree. They were never more than a few feet away from each other as they worked. Kisses and soft touches seemed to further solidify their bond, and their new path.

Soon Josh woke from his nap and Rick went to get him while Bear continued to wrap lights around the tree. They'd gotten most of the decorations up around the house, and, of course, his fiancé had been correct, it looked amazing. They'd not decorated the tree further than lights and garland. They'd agreed the rest would be done together as a family.

Ten minutes later his family appeared at the bottom of the stairs. Josh's eyes were wide, as he took in the decorations from his perch on his Rick's hip.

"Unk…unk, Christmas," Josh cheered while waving his stuffed dragon in the air.

"Yeah, big guy, Christmas," Bear agreed as he walked over, picked Josh out of Rick's arms, and showed Josh everything.

The three of them did a lap around the house because there wasn't a room untouched by an elf named Rick. Josh seemed to get more and more excited as the tour carried on. They wrapped up beside their Christmas tree. The only boxes left out contained the ornaments.

Bear set Josh down among the boxes. The breakable ornaments were all safely on the dining room table so that Josh could investigate without fear of demolishing anything. Rick and Bear intended that they would finish the tree together every year until Josh had a family of his own, and then they'd be included in the annual ritual.

The little guy began digging in, pulling one ornament out after the next until he was surrounded. Both Bear and Rick were down on their hands and knees making sure Josh saw every one of them.

"These go on the Christmas tree, Josh," Rick instructed, then picked up a wooden angel and placed it on the tree.

Josh was bright and got the hang of what to do quickly. After the boy had put all "his" ornaments around the tree, they lifted him to the top of the tree to put on more ornaments. Their laughter filled the room as Josh talked their ears off about reindeer as he made one jump from branch to branch.

They stopped decorating to eat dinner as the light outside slowly faded to night. Once the dishes were placed in the dishwasher they came back out to finish, Josh ready to go all over again. Part way through Rick returned to the kitchen to make them all hot chocolate with little marshmallows.

Finally, Rick opened the last box. It contained the angel Bear's sister Jenny had given them for their last Christmas together. Bear could feel the weight pressing down on his chest. He missed his sister. He held Josh a bit closer and took the angel from his fiancé's hands, his grief easy to see no matter how much Rick tried to hide it. Bear loved him so completely and times like this only reinforced that.

Josh touched the golden feathers with the tips of his chubby little fingers. Bear never wanted his nephew to forget Jenny and he would spend the rest of his life reminding her son what a wonderful woman she was. "This is Mommy's angel. Mommy gave this to us." Bear wasn't sure how Josh would react, if at all. It had been months since he'd woken up at night calling for her.

Bear could almost see his toddler brain trying to figure it out. Then suddenly he said, "Mommy loves me," before pointing to the picture Rick had framed and hung on the wall.

Every day he'd hear Rick talking about Jenny to Josh and point at the picture. Bear did it as well, but considering Rick was home full time, he had more of an impact on Josh. It did something to Bear knowing his love was doing everything to keep Jenny's memory alive for Josh.

"Yes, Mommy loves you very much," Rick was quick to say as Bear fought back tears.

He mouthed the words "thank you" to Rick before turning to Josh, saying, "Mommy gave that to us so that she would be with us every Christmas. But you know what I think, big guy?"

Josh looked up at Bear with the same blue eyes as Jenny and Bear had. "I think Mommy is here with us every day, not just Christmas, and she watches over you."

He knew Josh didn't completely understand what Bear was trying to explain but someday he would, and that's what mattered. Bear lifted Josh toward the top of the tree as Rick helped direct Josh what to do. Between the three of them, the angel managed to reach its perch for another season and they turned on the Christmas lights.

The effect was magical, exactly as Rick had intended. The tiny lights glowed cheerfully as the three sank onto the sectional in their normal positions, Bear in the middle with Rick and Josh on either side. Exactly where they belonged and where he could take care of them.

Then he turned on the TV to a Christmas special with Burl Ives narrating as a snowman, the show a classic Bear had grown up watching. He leaned back with his arms around his family and let himself fall into the Christmas magic his love had created.

Chapter Four

Jesse and Royce

"I think it's stunning, absolutely gorgeous. Johnny and Gabe will love it as the backdrop to their wedding," Nardo said before shooting another picture for the *Brighton Bugler*.

Jesse watched on as the young man shined. Nardo had come to Haven with his brother Tony and three more young men when they were rescued from a conversion therapy center in another state. When they'd arrived, Nardo had barely said a word. His older brother, Tony, spoke for him and Nardo had refused to leave his brother's side.

The mural renowned artist Randy Reynolds had painted on the wall in the large community center exuded joy. Jesse wasn't sure how Randy could make paint produce such strong emotions, but it was the man's innate talent, which he shared freely. The mural had been a gift from Shadow and Randy to celebrate The Safe Haven Center's Grand Opening.

"That should do it," Nardo said as he handed the camera back over to Mr. Weaver, the owner of the *Bugler*. He'd come in initially to take the shots himself, noticed Nardo's interest, showed him how the camera worked, and let the young man free.

Nardo looked nervous as Mr. Weaver reviewed the photos on the camera screen. A few moments passed until he looked up at Nardo and said, "You have an eye for this, son. These shots are well done." Then Mr. Weaver reached into his bag, pulled out a business card, and handed it to Nardo. "You give me a call after Christmas and we'll see where you might fit at the *Bugler*."

The young man held the card like it was the most precious thing he'd ever received. "Thank you, Mr. Weaver." Nardo looked over and smiled at Jesse before running to his brother, who was watching from the doors to the small café that they'd built. God he loved Brighton and the people that called it home.

It was these moments that drove Jesse to work harder to ensure as many people as possible had a safe place to go and a place to thrive.

"Have I told you yet how proud I am of you today?" Royce asked as he wrapped his arms around Jesse's waist from behind. His strong arms always made Jesse feel safe and loved even though he outweighed his partner by over sixty-five pounds and stood a few inches taller. Royce was his rock.

"Only once or twice, but I like hearing it. Along with 'I love you,'" Jesse teased as he turned around to face his amazing boyfriend—the man who had stood right beside him through everything that had been thrown at them, even when his family had tried to make Jesse disappear.

"Well then, I must rectify this immediately. I love you, Jesse, and I'm proud of you." Royce's voice was strong and sure, guaranteeing that Jesse never had to worry about his man's feelings.

"Proud of us. We did this together, don't you forget that." Jesse leaned forward and kissed the person who meant everything to him. "Without you, none of this would have ever been possible. Without you, everything could have been taken from me…even my life."

"We're in this together. We're a team, a family." Royce kept his voice low so that their conversation wouldn't be overheard. "Your old family is locked away for a long time. No one will ever hurt you again."

Jesse laid his head against Royce's and simply enjoyed the moment in his partner's arms before the next Haven issue required their attention. As if he'd portended it, a heavy can crashed to the floor somewhere behind him. When Jesse and Royce turned to see what had happened, they found Simon, one of the other young men who'd been brought to Haven from the conversion center, standing over a spilt can of white paint on their newly polished concrete floor. He still had the brush in his hand. He had been helping paint the trim around the doors and windows of the offices.

Simon looked ready to break down or run, either was possible, and Jesse was quick to respond. "It's okay, man. No worries. It was an accident."

Unfortunately, that didn't seem to help and sadly Jesse completely understood. The people coming here for help and safety had been through so much trauma already that they could have fear responses and flashbacks at any time. Simon's hand was shaking so hard that Jesse wasn't sure how he was still holding the brush.

The few people in the large room had stopped what they were doing, and were now staring at Simon. *Not helping.* "Simon, it's okay. Everyone else, please step out for a moment."

As the room cleared, Jesse approached Simon slowly with his hands out in front of him. He tried to make himself as small as possible, which was a feat in itself considering how big he was. He and Simon had spent a fair bit of time talking since he'd arrived and Jesse hoped that would be enough for the scared man to give him a chance.

"No one is upset with you. No one is going to hurt you. I promise you I would never let that happen. It was an accident. We'll clean it up and start over." Jesse kept up the one-sided conversation as he got closer, and it seemed to be working. At least, Simon's hand had stopped shaking.

"B-but I ruined it. It's all my fault. I have to be severely punished or how will you know that I'm sorry?" Simon asked in such a sad voice it nearly broke Jesse's heart. What this poor young man must have gone through.

"I know you're sorry, Simon. It was an accident. You didn't do it on purpose, did you?"

Simon was quick to answer. "No. I would never do that. You've given me so much."

Jesse knelt down beside the puddle of white paint and righted the can. "See, I knew you didn't. You've been such an asset to me since you've arrived here. You're always helping out, showing how much you care about Haven."

The abject fear in Simon's eyes finally melted away and he looked at the mess on the floor with new eyes. "How will we clean this up?" Jesse let out a breath he hadn't known he was holding.

"With these," Jesse said as he got up, went to the back room and then came out with an arm full of paper towels and a garbage can. "They'll do the trick, no worries, and we'll help you."

Simon looked back and forth between Jesse, who was still kneeling on the floor and Royce, who was standing at the ready. "Ookay," he agreed, still looking unsure, as if waiting for the other shoe to fall.

Royce handed out the towels and both he and Simon knelt down and joined Jesse as they wiped up the paint. Simon seemed like he was starting to believe nothing bad would happen to him, and one by one, people began returning inside the building and joined in the cleanup. Nardo and Tony brought out cleaning supplies to use on the floor after the paint had been cleared away. Jesse wasn't one hundred percent sure if the oil-based paint would mar the flooring and didn't care if it did. It could be replaced. Providing Simon with the safety and security he needed was more important.

With everyone's help, the mess was cleaned away in no time, and surprisingly with very little damage to the floor. Jesse took the paintbrush out of Simon's hand, went to the storage room, and got a new can of paint and a brush. When he returned Simon was back to looking unsure even though Royce was talking to him calmly.

Jesse handed the can of paint and new brush to Simon without saying a word. Simon would have to decide if he wanted to pick himself up and try again. Jesse stood silently for a few moments before he put the can and brush down on the floor. He hoped Simon would take that next step and as he was getting ready to walk away, he was shocked when Simon wrapped his arms around him and said, "Thank you."

As quickly as he'd grabbed him, Simon released Jesse, picked up his supplies, and walked back to where he originally had been painting. Jesse watched on with pride. Simon had made it over another hurdle.

A sense of belonging washed over Jesse, He was convinced that this was the path his grandfather had wanted him to take when he'd left Jesse the farm.

He could feel Royce's presence beside him, his rock, always and forever.

***

Hours later Royce was in his home office staring at the nondescript cardboard box at his feet. Hesitating wasn't in his character, and right at that moment he felt unsure, making him even more frustrated.

"How long are you going to stare at it?" Jesse asked from the open doorway. "Tell me what has you so bothered, love, and I'll try to help."

Jesse walked into the room and sat in the chair opposite Royce, placing the box between them. He leaned back in his old leather high-back chair and noted the concern and confusion on his lover's face. That wouldn't do. It was time to man up. He got out of his chair and sat on the carpeted floor before motioning Jesse to join him.

"Come sit with me, love."

The big man could move fast when he wanted to. Jesse was on the floor by Royce's side almost immediately. He wrapped his arm around Jesse and pulled him close. He preferred having his partner as near to him as possible. He didn't know how Jesse would respond to what Royce wanted to do. Would he become angry or defensive? Would he be hurt by it and see it as a slap in his face? Even though Jesse had been accepting of Royce's past before, it did not mean there wasn't a chance of Royce pushing him too hard.

"Jesse, I have something I'd like to ask you and I want you to answer me honestly. If you have a concern about it, then I will never bring it up again. I won't have you upset and I don't want to hurt you in any way."

As he expected, that got Jesse's full attention. "Is something wrong?"

"No, no, love. It has something to do with my past," Royce tried to explain but wasn't sure where to start.

Jesse cupped Royce's cheek, sending warmth throughout his body. "Whatever it is, Royce, know that I love you. Ask me and we can figure it out together."

"Maybe I should show you first." Royce said before opening the box and pulling the first wrapped figure out of safekeeping, where he'd placed them a lifetime ago.

One by one, he removed the bubble wrap surrounding the figures and buildings until a small town began to take shape. He touched every carved piece with the same care he'd used to pack it away for what he thought would be forever. Now, things had changed. His life was filled with love and purpose again.

"Is that Bear's diner?" Jesse asked in what sounded like awe.

"Yeah," Royce answered as he placed the gazebo down beside the park swings.

"The firehouse and town hall, too. It looks like the entire main street is here," Jesse gushed at the discovery. "It's beautiful. Who made these?"

"Daniel." One word, yet so many emotions. Royce's first husband and high school sweetheart had died many years ago in an automobile accident. That was when he'd packed a large part of his life away along with any hope for the future. That had changed the day Royce had walked into the diner and saw Jesse behind the counter for the first time.

"They're stunning. He was really talented," Jesse said as he reached for the diner, but stopping short. "Is it okay if I touch them?"

"Of course." Royce watched as the man he intended to spend the rest of his life with carefully examined the creations made by the man with whom Royce had begun his life. He watched Jesse closely for any sign of discomfort or concern, but saw none.

"There's the Brighton Christmas Tree, and there are Christmas decorations in the shop windows. This is the whole town decked out for Christmas," Jesse said as he became more excited.

"That's what I wanted to ask you. We used to put this up on the mantel every Christmas and Daniel would always make a new one every year. Don't feel as though you have to say yes, truly, but I was hoping we could display them again."

Jesse set the town hall down and took Royce into his arms. "Sweetheart, of course we can. I know you still love Daniel."

Royce didn't want to upset Jesse but he couldn't lie. "I do."

"That's the way it's supposed to be. You and Daniel loved each other for many years and probably would still be together now if it hadn't been for the accident. I know this, but that doesn't mean you love me any less. I want you to remember and celebrate the love the two of you shared. He will always be a part of you, the same as I am. Your heart is certainly big enough, and I don't mind sharing it with your first love."

Royce could only stare at the smiling man in front of him. How had he been afraid of Jesse's response? He should have known better and now he felt a touch of shame for thinking the worse. "I'm sorry, honey."

"There's nothing to be sorry about. You were worried because you didn't want to hurt me or make me feel bad. I'm lucky to have someone as thoughtful as you," Jesse explained before giving him a kiss that Royce quickly dominated, causing his man to moan. "None of that until we get the Brighton Christmas Town set up."

The two of them placed the figures back into the box and headed for their living room. Jesse began to clear off the mantel as Royce continued to unwrap the remaining figures of the town.

"Oh wait, I have something that will work perfectly," Jesse announced before leaving the room and heading down the hallway to their spare bedroom.

Royce couldn't wipe the smile from his face even if he wanted to, which he didn't. Most of the town's people liked to refer to Jesse as the gentle giant, and for good reason. The scope of the man's love and understanding never ceased to amaze Royce.

"Here it is," Jesse hollered before he came racing back down the hall with something that looked like sparkling cotton pressed into thick sheets. "I was out buying more wrapping paper and I saw this and had to have it. I didn't know what the hell I was going to do with it but now I know. It was meant to be."

Jesse spread the cotton over the top of their wooden mantel before reaching for the diner and placing it on top. "Snow."

"You're brilliant. It looks perfect and at least one of the Brightons will have a white Christmas," Royce said as he set out the firehouse and police station.

For the next forty minutes, they set up the town. They even went so far as to take pieces of the cotton and drape them over rooftops, making it looked like it had recently snowed. They turned off all the house lights, and sat on the plush area rug with only the glow of the Christmas tree lights to see the replica town.

"I bet I could make small streetlights that actually light for up and down main street," Jesse offered before he began biting his lip. "That is if it's okay with you. I don't want to...."

Whatever else his man was about to say was cut off when Royce took Jesse's lips in a blistering kiss full of teeth and tongues. Royce pushed Jesse onto his back and followed him down without breaking their kiss. So many emotions were racing through Royce's body, from joy to a newfound peace. But more than anything, at that moment Royce *needed* to make love to his partner.

"I would love it if you made streetlights for the town. I want a part of you involved with that piece of Daniel I carry in my heart," Royce assured him before diving back in for an even deeper kiss as he began unbuttoning Jesse's shirt.

Royce could feel his lover's hard cock through the denim of Jesse's jeans and had the intense urge to taste his smooth, salty skin. "Clothes off, babe," Royce said as he stood and began stripping.

He watched as Jesse shimmied out of his jeans and boxers, his shirt and socks soon joined the growing pile of clothing. Royce couldn't help but groan at the delectable sight in front of him.

Jesse's sandy blond hair stood out in all directions from running his hands through it, while his dark brown eyes pulled Royce even deeper into whatever spell the man had over him. His tanned muscular body was a work of art, and Royce crawled over his man, intent on getting his taste.

Royce began licking and sucking his way up Jesse's inner thighs, tormenting him by getting close to the prize, but heading back down to start all over again. The big man shook with need. Jesse reached for his cock but Royce had other things in mind. "Don't touch yourself. You belong to me and will not come until I allow you."

Royce had always been the dominant man in their relationship, and today was no exception as he watched Jesse's hands rise above his head to lie flat on the floor. His lover's breathing sped up as he moaned his agreement. Because of his size people always mistook him as the dominant partner, especially in bed, but it couldn't be further from the truth. Jesse thrived and was happiest in a more submissive role and Royce was more than happy to oblige.

"That's it, Jesse, I'll give you what you need," Royce said, and without warning, he took Jesse's hard cock down his throat and swallowed. His throat muscles squeezed and massaged Jesse's shaft repeatedly as he cried out. But he didn't come, which made Royce happy. He intended to give his amazing man an earth-shaking orgasm.

Jesse was babbling in between moans, exactly where Royce wanted him. He took the bottle of lube they kept hidden under the couch cushions and began circling Jesse's hole with slippery fingers. Not once did he release his hold on Jesse's cock as he continued licking and sucking him down.

One finger than another slid in and out of his lover, giving Jesse a prostate massage like nothing he'd ever had before. Royce took his time stretching and rubbing, every moan driving him forward.

"Honey, please…please, I need you inside me," Jesse begged as he pulled his legs back.

Royce released his prize with one final lick and brought his body over the top of his needy partner. Jesse watched every move he made. His pupils were blown wide and his face flushed, heightening his incredible beauty. Royce lined his cock up with Jesse's hole, allowing the head to enter his lover before leaning down and taking Jesse in a slow, passionate kiss. He released all of his emotions to run freely through that kiss before pushing himself farther in until his balls touched Jesse's ass.

They both groaned at the intense pleasure they were sharing, and neither had looked away from the other the entire time. "You are so beautiful, Jesse. Every part of you deserves to be cherished, and I intend to do that for the rest of my life."

Jesse reached up and ran his fingers through Royce's hair. "I love you so much."

Royce couldn't hold back any longer and flexed his hips before pulling back and driving forward again. They set a furious pace, both lost to their passion. The colorful Christmas lights bathed them in a warm glow while their bodies joined together as their hearts already had.

Jesse's moans and gasps told Royce that his lover was close to losing control, and his fight not to come without permission. He would never do anything cruel to his man. Sex play was supposed to enhance the experience, not diminish it or denigrate his lover.

"Come for me," Royce commanded as he wrapped his hand around Jesse's hard cock and pumped him at the same speed as his own cock was driving in and out of his lover.

Jesse froze for a fraction of a second before roaring his release to the ceiling as pulse after pulse of come splashed onto his muscled stomach. His channel squeezed Royce tight and he fought to slide as deeply as possible before being overcome by his own release.

His ears were still ringing for several moments as they both gasped for air while tangled in each other's arms. Royce gently pulled out and lay beside his lover before reaching up to the couch and pulling a knitted blanket over the both of them. Jesse had a peaceful smile on his face and Royce couldn't look away from the sight.

"Royce?"

"Yes, babe."

"You know how much you mean to me, right?" Jesse asked before opening his eyes to look up at him. His eyes said it all without him uttering a word. The powerful love in those brown depths was unmistakable.

Royce ran his fingers through Jesse's hair and answered, "Yes. You don't have to worry that anything was ever left unsaid. As I hope it is the same when I look at you."

Jesse's smile lit up his face. "Yeah, I know."

Royce leaned down and slowly kissed the man who had shown him he could still live even after tragedy. He lay back onto the carpeting, tucked a throw pillow under his head while Jesse settled his head on Royce's chest, and covered him with his leg. Soon Jesse's breathing evened out, his handsome face aglow with the reds, yellows, and oranges of the Christmas tree lights.

For the first time in a very long time, Royce looked upon the Christmas town as a work in progress. Ever evolving, ever changing, and simply because one great love had begun it didn't mean another couldn't join in and help it grow.

The town would look amazing with streetlights.

Chapter Five

Coop and Matthew

"Move it two inches to the east," Matthew repeated into his walkie-talkie.

The view on his monitor changed ever so slightly but now it included the rear entrance and the entire northeast side of the building.

"Perfect," he confirmed. "Bolt it in."

Matthew flipped to another screen before rechecking if the camera was in the right position. Out of the over one hundred cameras they were installing, they'd had to adjust only two. He'd take that as a victory. Months of preparation to secure Haven was finally coming to fruition, and Matthew couldn't have been happier with the results.

It meant something knowing that in any small way he had helped to make the people coming to the Haven safe. He rubbed the small scar on his right cheek, a constant reminder that evil did exist. Matthew pushed those thoughts far away and concentrated on the systems in front of him. He clicked to the cameras in the pool area, which were still being positioned, to find the sexiest man Matthew had ever seen, Coop.

His man was helping move bags of concrete over to the mixer as the crew worked on the finishing details of the pool. When they weren't away on missions, the Sentinel team had been pitching in around the new center. Matthew couldn't help himself and zoomed in on his partner. He watched as Coop's muscles flexed and bulged with every move he made. Matthew liked to joke that Coop was built like a Greek god, but in truth he absolutely was, no joke.

Matthew picked up his cellphone and pushed the button with Coop's handsome face on it. He watched as Coop pulled out his phone and smiled wide, giving Matthew a bird's-eye view into how happy Coop was when Matthew called. That left a warm feeling in his chest, and while he knew the big guy loved him, there was no harm in being reassured.

"Hi, beautiful. What's up?" Coop's deep voice touched him like an actual caress.

"Finishing confirming the cameras are in the correct locations and then I found something I couldn't take my eyes off of," Matthew teased as Coop began looking around until he found the camera and stared straight at him.

"You little peeping Tom you." Coop laughed as he waved at the camera Matthew was using.

"You can't blame me when the view is this good."

The system was so accurate that Matthew could see Coop's cheeks turning red. "You almost done up there?"

"I'll be another hour tops."

"Okay, we can stop at the diner on our way home," Coop suggested. "I heard some of the contractors mentioning that Travis had fried chicken on the menu as today's special."

Travis made the best chicken in town. Matthew didn't know what it was that the man did differently, but whatever it was he, like the rest of the town, hoped Travis kept doing it. "Can we take it to go?"

Matthew watched as Coop's smile widened. "You want to have a picnic?"

"Definitely. I'll come find you when I'm done, but can you do me one favor?"

"Of course, beautiful. What do you need?"

"For you to turn around slowly and show me that gorgeous ass of yours." Matthew would not forego the opportunity to zoom into that perfect peach-shaped tush. "Oh yeah, that's the stuff."

Coop laughed as he turned around anyway and gave Matthew a little shake before saying, "Love you, you pervert."

"Love you too, Coop," Matthew replied before hanging up and switching to another camera.

As he continued his triple check of the completed systems, Matthew couldn't help but think how much his life had changed. Without Coop, he'd still be in his one-bedroom condo in San Diego working behind the scenes on whatever mission he'd chosen, or working on munitions he was busy creating. Never out in the open or part of a team.

Now he was a Sentinel, contract and all, and not simply because he was with Coop. He'd travelled further than he ever thought he'd go, learned how to defend himself and to get control over his clumsy self. Although, on occasion he was known to trip over air, those instances were now rare. Well, if you didn't count the lip of the shower on Tuesday, or the potted plant on Friday.

Once he was done with his camera check, he left and locked the security room before heading in search of the man who'd laid claim to his heart, not to mention body. He walked along a path surrounded by flowers and trees. Jesse had said he wanted this place to feel homey and loved, so now gardens could be found everywhere. A noise caught his attention, causing Matthew to stop and listen more closely.

Snip…snip… Matthew followed the sound down a side path until he came face-to-back with Tommy. Tommy was one of the three young men freed from the conversion therapy center and had been brought to Haven. He was using small pruning shears on a shrub that stood about three feet tall. Even from where Matthew was standing, he could make out the shape of a birdbath.

"Hello, Tommy, what are you up to today?" Matthew asked, causing the poor man to jump in surprise. At least he hadn't screamed. That would have brought the cavalry running. "It's okay, it's only me."

"I'm sorry, Mr. Whitton, I didn't hear you coming." Tommy hid the shears behind his leg as if what he was doing could get him into trouble.

"Tommy, what's up? Is something wrong?" 'Cause if there was Matthew would fix it or have Coop do it. Since his arrival, Tommy had been kind and courteous to everyone.

The young man brought the shears back out and showed Matthew. "I promise I didn't steal them."

"Of course you haven't," Matthew assured.

"I borrowed them from the garden shed. I would have put them right back."

Matthew's heart broke for what this poor man had been through to fear everything and everyone. "Come sit with me, let's talk," he said before leading Tommy to a nearby concrete bench.

"I know you wouldn't steal them. I believe you."

Tommy looked shocked but he did his best to hide it. "You believe me?"

"Yeah, sure."

"But you don't even really know me."

"From what I have seen so far, I have no reason not to trust you," Matthew explained. "Now, tell me what you're creating?"

Tommy lowered his head before answering. "A mess."

"I don't know about that. Is it going to be a birdbath?"

Tommy's eyes lit up. "It is."

"Were you always interested in art?"

"Art?"

"Yeah, topiary. Living sculpture."

"I didn't know it was a form of art, but I used to do it with my mother when I was small, before she left."

Matthew refused to let the sadness he felt inside for the young man show. Poor guy, working alone to keep his memories of his mother alive was heartbreaking. "Well, I have a good friend named Sam who does this as well. Here, I'll show you some pictures." He reached into his pocket, pulled out his cell, and opened his phone's photo file. One by one, he flipped through the pictures of the topiaries surrounding the old Victorian house at the compound. Tommy looked on in complete fascination.

There was no way Matthew could simply let this go, that wasn't his style. "I could bring you out sometime to see them if you want."

"Really?" Tommy couldn't hide his excitement, making Matthew smile.

"Sure, and maybe I could ask Sam to be there when you visit. It would be good to get two artists together to talk over things. Me, I don't have a clue other than they're beautiful." Matthew's heart went out to Tommy, alone in the world, knowing he was tossed aside without a care for his safety. Matthew knew what that felt like. He had no doubt Sam would want to help as well.

"That would be awesome. Thank you." The change from when Matthew first saw Tommy to now would make someone believe he'd given him something priceless. All Matthew wanted to do was make the young man smile.

"Okay. I'll be here at Haven often and we'll work out a good time for everyone to visit." He stood and turned to the soon to be birdbath and said, "You can show him this when you're finished. Have a good day, Tommy."

"Thank you, Mr. Whitton."

Matthew retraced his steps until he was back on the original path and found Coop waiting there for him. His lover wrapped those muscled arms around him and lifted Matthew into the air. "There you are," he muttered before taking Matthew's lips in a passionate kiss, wiping away any residual sadness he was still carrying.

Matthew knew how lucky he was to have a life with this amazing man.

***

Coop knew how lucky he was to have a life with this beautiful man.

They stopped by the diner on their way home and picked up two fried chicken dinners. Mrs. Walker had the evening off so the team had to fend for themselves. The moment they walked through the door Matthew ran to find Sam. Coop had heard about Tommy, and was sure Matthew wouldn't let the young man down. Coop's man always kept his promises. After Matthew had shared, he shut it down. Coop had learned his partner preferred doing things without praise. Matthew had told him a ton of times that what Matthew did was simple acts of kindness that everyone should engage in, nothing to be thanked for.

Matthew was one of a kind, like his multicolored eyes, and Coop had no idea what he did before this man had come into his life. Well, other than the fact that he'd been a love 'em and leave 'em kinda guy, but once he met Matthew, those days were over.

Coop had placed their food into an insulated bag to keep it warm while he quickly stripped and jumped into the shower. The steam floated around him, fogging up the glass. He sensed the moment he was no longer alone and waited for his man to join him. He didn't have to wait long.

Matthew's hands explored Coop's back before wrapping around him from behind. Coop loved having Matthew close and twisted in his arms so that he was now facing his man.

"Hi there, lover. Want me to scrub your back?" Coop asked.

"And my sides and we can't forget about my front. I need your personal attention." Matthew played along.

"Hmmm, I'll have to see what I can do for you, beautiful," Coop teased as he pulled Matthew even closer before claiming his lips.

After a few moments, he had Matthew moaning into the kiss while rubbing his hard cock against Coop's leg. This was how he loved to see his partner, wet and needy. Coop could definitely work with this. He reached down, covered Matthew's ass cheeks with large hands, and squeezed before lifting his love so that they were now eye-to-eye.

Matthew wiggled, desperately trying to find any friction on his cock. Coop worked his way down his lover's neck, licking and sucking hard enough to leave marks as he went. The feel of Matthew's hard cock and balls rubbing up and down his abdomen made his own swollen balls throb with need.

"That's it, beautiful, take what you need from me," Coop groaned as he reached for the waterproof lube.

Moments later, he was circling Matthew's tight hole, loosening the muscles enough to allow him in. His first finger slid in deep and Matthew's moans grew louder in the tiled enclosure. Coop pressed Matthew's back against the wall and sunk another finger in beside the first.

The stunning man in his arms began to cry out and soon Coop had three fingers in, making sure his lover was stretched.

"Ready, baby?" Coop growled. He was barely holding on at this point and needed to bury himself deep inside Matthew.

"Please hurry."

That was all the assurance Coop needed as he lined the sensitive head of his cock up with Matthew's waiting hole. Slowly and with great care he pushed forward until his balls were snug to his lover's ass. He groaned at the tight heat squeezing his cock as muscles spasmed around him.

Coop took Matthew's red, swollen lips in another deep kiss, desperate to show his man how much he loved him. Wanting to give him everything, wanting him to know every part of Coop belonged to Matthew. He no longer feared love, now he felt more secure and solid with it than without. Matthew had given this to him.

He flexed his hips, driving a bit deeper before pulling out. On his way back in he made sure to rub Matthew's prostate until his lover began babbling between moans. Coop loved it when he was able to drive Matthew to the point of pure bliss.

"I-I'm... come," Matthew moaned.

Coop immediately took hold of his partner's cock and began pumping him long and hard. With a dip of his nail into his lover's slit, Coop felt Matthew's muscles tighten before he cried out and painted Coop's stomach in warm come. The feel of Matthew coming apart in Coop's arms did nothing for his stamina, but he pushed on until several moments later Coop came deep inside the man who had made his life whole.

Matthew clung to him as they both fought to catch their breath. Coop had braced himself against the tile, never wanting his beauty to slip out of his arms. Once he was sure Matthew could stand on his own two feet again, Coop set him down and began washing him. The dreamy smile on his partner's face never ceased to fill Coop with a smug pride. He'd put that smile there.

"How are you feeling?" Coop asked as he began rinsing off Matthew.

"Happy, relaxed, loved...there's more but you get the gist." Matthew punctuated every emotion with a kiss to Coop's chest.

"Perfect. Right where I want you." Coop finished washing himself before leading his partner out of the shower and drying him off.

They put on their matching robes, a gift from Matthew, and headed back into the bedroom to unpack their picnic. Shadow laid a blanket on the floor in front of the gas fireplace before turning it on. The glow from the flames made everything more intimate. Matthew set out the plates and cutlery while he dug the takeout containers from the insulated bag. Thankfully, everything was still warm.

Matthew pulled a bottle of wine out of their new wine fridge they'd installed in their bedroom. Private picnics had been their thing since the beginning. The two would sit cuddled together on their ever growing stack of pillows in front of the fire with a glass of wine a few times a week to wind down and share the day's events. Coop reached into the bottom dresser drawer for the last and most important piece of what he wanted to discuss with Matthew this evening. He hoped he wasn't pushing their relationship too quickly, but couldn't help wanting to move forward.

"What do you have there?" Matthew asked as Coop set the cardboard tube on the floor beside his plate.

"A question."

That got Matthew's interest. "A question in a tube?"

"Yeah, but I thought we should wait until after we've eaten."

"Not a chance, big guy. I'm not waiting. What's your question?"

Coop thought about it for a moment before agreeing it might be best to get this out of the way first. He opened the lid on the tube and slid the rolled-up paper out and onto the floor in front of Matthew. With one final curious look at Coop, Matthew unrolled the papers and got his first look at a dream close to Coop's heart.

He didn't say a word, he simply allowed Matthew to look through the pages without his commentary. His lover took his time reviewing each page until he came to the end and looked up at Coop.

"How long have you had these drawings?"

"Years. I drew them up quite a while ago."

"And what do you wish to do with them?"

"What I want *us* to do with these blueprints is build it. You know, once you've had a chance to look over it and make any changes you want."

"You want to build a house with me?"

"No, I want to build a home with you. More than anything. There's a beautiful plot of land I want to take you to see and—"

Whatever else he was going to say was cut off when Matthew dove into Coop's arms, repeating the same word over and over again between kisses.

"Yes."

Chapter Six

Gabe and Johnny

Johnny held his phone closer to his ear so that he could hear over Gabe and Lucy's playtime in the center of their living room. The two were having a tea party, and for the life of him, he couldn't figure out how tea could be so loud. But he loved every minute of it.

"Hold on, Saint. I'm walking outside onto the patio," Johnny said to his brother, Frank, better known as Saint, who was waiting on the other end of the line. He didn't know why his brother was reaching out to him after being absent from his life for years. This sounded like he wanted to talk about more than coming to the wedding.

"It's okay, Johnny, I don't mind holding," Saint replied happily, which was even more puzzling.

He closed the patio door behind him and stepped out into the cool night breeze. "Okay, I'm outside now. What were you saying?"

"I was letting you know that I'm going to be in Brighton next week and I'm hoping we could get together," Saint explained.

Johnny could hear the uncertainty in his brother's voice. "Is something wrong? Are you okay?" Johnny may have lost track of his brother for a few years, but Saint was still his older brother. He loved him even if he had followed their father into medicine, plastic surgery particularly, for money, not healing.

"Nothing's wrong, little brother. I would really like to see you and your family." Saint hesitated. "I've missed you."

Johnny couldn't hear any dissembling in his voice, which surprised him. Giving a mental shrug, he replied, "Okay, when will you be getting in?"

He heard his brother let out a breath before answering. "I'll be in town on the fifteenth before I continue on out to Los Angeles after your wedding."

"What's in Los Angeles?" Johnny asked, considering the medical practice was based in New York.

"I'll catch you up with the whole of it when I see you, little brother. Thank you for agreeing to see me and inviting me to your wedding."

"You're my brother. Of course I want you there." He'd always wanted his brother there, even when Saint had pulled away.

"I know we haven't been close over the last few years, but I'd like to change that if I can."

"I'd like that as well, Saint."

"Good. I'll call you when I get into town." Saint sounded much happier than he had at the beginning of their conversation. "Love you, bro," he said before the line went dead.

Johnny stood there for several minutes, staring at the phone in his hand. He couldn't remember the last time his brother said that he loved him.

Something was seriously wrong.

Chapter Seven

Travis and Bo

The flow of charcoal from his pencil made the lines darker than the softest graphite pencil ever could. There was always something about that first stroke of pencil to paper, or paint to canvas, that sent excitement rushing through his veins. Add to that the fact that this wasn't some ordinary drawing. This one was special. Travis had drawn and redrawn this design over twenty times by now and he wouldn't stop until it was perfect.

Late afternoon sunshine streamed into his studio that Bo had created for him in the house they now shared. His boyfriend was out back working in his gardens, giving Travis the time he needed to perfect what he was creating, then scanning it, and sending it on over to Olivia to trace for her stencil. The design incorporated Bo's work life as a police officer and Travis's as an artist, combining both passions as they had done in their private lives.

Bo's badge stood proudly in the center of the piece with different aspects of their lives together peeking out from behind it. Travis's sable paintbrush, flowers from Bo's garden, the badge number of Bo's first partner on the force who was killed in a shootout, the name of the soup kitchen where Travis and his dad had helped before his father's death, and the Mason family crest. If Travis had to say so himself, the piece was beautiful. There were to be two versions of the drawing, one larger than the other, otherwise, they were identical.

His mind wandered as he worked, which happened often when he was creating. Many months had passed since he'd moved in with Bo, and every day he woke up in that wonderful man's arms. Travis reached back and scratched at the small rash he'd gotten rolling around in the grass in their backyard without his shirt on. Bo had a picnic set up for them when he'd gotten off shift at the diner, and it was a good thing they had a tall fence and mature trees.

Amazing to begin with was Travis had taken off his shirt while outside. He'd never have considered doing it in the past even though they were alone and away from prying eyes. It was yet another step forward. As he scratched, he was careful not to push too hard on the raised scars left behind when his skin had burned in the fire. Sometimes they could become sensitive.

For the first time in Travis's life, his appearance wasn't his defining feature. His scars didn't rule his thoughts as they used to, and with Bo, family and friends, and with the help of Dr. Gordon, Travis was rebuilding his life, and for the first time planning for the future.

Hours passed before he was finally satisfied. Travis scanned the final work and sent it off. It was time to find the man he loved. Travis stepped out onto the back patio in time to see Bo closing the garden shed before walking toward him. The blinding smile on Bo's face did wonders for Travis. He was the one who made Bo smile like that, and he would do anything to keep it that way. Travis watched transfixed as Bo's muscles flexed as he moved. *Yep, all mine.*

"Hey, babe, all done?" Bo asked as he stepped onto the patio and took Travis into his arms.

Travis snaked his hands over Bo's wide chest and up around his neck. "Yep, already sent it off."

"Excited?"

"Definitely. You?"

"Oh yeah, I've been wanting to do this for a while now," Bo replied before he began kissing his way down Travis's neck, almost distracting him.

"None of that quite yet. We still have to take a drive out to Haven to okay the installation," Travis reminded his insistent partner.

Bo playfully growled but pulled back. "But I want to get you naked."

"And you will, later," Travis assured.

Funny how such a big man could pout as effectively as his goddaughter, who was only two. "Come on, it won't take long, and then you can play when we soak in the tub."

That brought Bo's smile back and soon enough they were in the truck and on the road to the new addition to Brighton, Safe Haven. In only a few more weeks they'd all be celebrating Bo's cousin, Gabe, and Johnny's wedding at the Center. With all the anticipation leading up to the event, it felt like the whole town would be there to celebrate.

Bo held his hand as Travis drove them out to the site that would be officially dedicated in seven days. Along with a phalanx of Brighton residents, Jesse and Royce had worked hard to make this happen. In all his years spent on the streets, Travis had never seen anything like Brighton. The town reminded him of what everyone imagined the ideal small town in America looked like, with the bonus of everyday technology and convenience, and an overall attitude of acceptance and tolerance.

They pulled into the recently paved parking lot with fresh yellow lines marking each parking spot. Everything was so new, and every attention to detail had been employed. It was an exciting time for the town. Bo walked around the truck and came to the driver's side to retake Travis's hand and lead him toward the main building. He couldn't help rub his shoulder against Bo as they walked. If he could, he'd be in constant contact with his man. Bo smiled down at him before pulling Travis even closer. *Yeah, I'm a lucky man.*

They walked into the foyer of Haven, and Travis was overwhelmed by what stood dead center in a place of honor. Three pieces of his artwork, large, medium, and small, hung behind glass with lights artfully arranged to highlight his paintings. Travis had donated the set of three images he'd painted of downtown Brighton to the Haven, but he never thought they'd be hung here like this. In all honesty, Travis thought they might be put up in the offices not displayed like actual artwork.

"It is artwork, sweetheart," Bo said, and Travis realized he must have said that last part aloud. "You are talented, and I'll keep saying it until it gets through."

The large painting depicted downtown, with its shops and flowers, street signs and lights. The image had been ingrained in his mind since the day he'd walked to Keith's art store for the first time. The medium-size painting was of the diner, the first place he'd called home since he turned eighteen. The smallest painting was of the flowers in Bo's gardens where they'd had their first date.

Below the paintings was a picture of Travis they must have gotten from Bo. Above the paintings was Travis's name in bold gold lettering. Underneath it, written in quotation was, "Dedicated to all those starting over and finding their own path. You will always find a home here."

Travis felt tears rolling down his cheeks but he was powerless to stop them. As Bo took him into his arms, Travis knew that his father was looking down on him with pride.

***

Bo sat back in the leather chair and laid his head against the headrest. The buzzing sound coming from another room confirmed that they were busy in the shop today. He wasn't nervous. He was overjoyed to be doing this with the man he loved. While Olivia prepared herself, Travis sat in the chair right by Bo's side, staring down at his own forearm with a wide smile. Bo heard someone groan from down the hall but nothing could pierce the happiness going on in this room.

Olivia pulled on her black latex gloves and smiled down at Bo. "Ready?"

"Definitely." Bo couldn't help his excitement.

Travis took hold of his hand and stared straight into Bo's eyes as Olivia leaned over to ink the first line. The pain from the needle was instantaneous but nothing he couldn't tolerate. The design Travis had drawn was breathtaking, and seeing a part of him inked onto his lover's body was almost perfect. Perfect would be after his own larger version of the tattoo was completed on his left pectoral muscle.

Bo had remembered Travis telling him that he used to design a new tattoo whenever he made it through another surgery. He stopped the day his mother had kicked him out after his father died. Bo had wanted to celebrate their union and asked Travis to create something for the two of them to share. The joy he'd seen today when Travis sat for his tattoo was worth anything and everything Bo had.

"You okay?" Travis asked as they stared at one another, never breaking contact.

"I'm doing fine, sweetheart. Are you happy with yours?" Bo thought he'd change the subject because for some odd reason Travis was great at getting a tattoo, but watching Bo get one was another matter. He looked ready to faint.

Travis looked down at his arm before gushing, "It's perfect."

"It is. Absolutely perfect, just like you."

Travis blushed as Bo had hoped he would before continuing with a conversation that he hoped was distracting Travis. Even when a particularly dark spot became tender, Bo didn't change his tone or facial expression. By the time Olivia was finished, they'd pretty much talked about and decided their entire holiday schedule. He looked down to see his new tattoo but Olivia wasn't done.

She cleaned the area and motioned for Bo to stand so he could get his first look at his chest. The tattoo spanned the width of his left pectoral muscle. Its bold lines flowed throughout the design, tying everything together in one stunning piece of art.

"Do you like it?" Travis asked, and Bo could hear the uncertainty in his lover's voice.

"It's breathtaking." Bo wasn't simply saying that to make Travis happy. It was one hundred percent truth. "You're amazing."

Bo pulled Travis close to his side and both stood looking into the mirror at their matching tattoos. He couldn't help the feeling of pride it gave him to have one of Travis's artworks over his heart. This was another step forward in their relationship while building their lives together, and he couldn't have been happier.

They held hands as they walked out of the shop and headed toward the diner. Bo wished he could walk around shirtless to show off his tattoo but that wouldn't do for a public servant of the community. He looked down at Travis who was beaming with happiness, and Bo knew he'd do everything to keep him that way as often as possible.

"You didn't even squirm," Travis said proudly. "You're amazing."

"I don't know. I hear getting a tattoo on a fleshy part of skin is less painful than boney areas like your forearm." Bo was quick to mention not wanting Travis to feel less for moving a bit.

"Yeah, I've heard that before too," Travis agreed. "Maybe they're right."

"I'm guessing they are. Now for our celebratory dinner. Are you sure you don't want to go to one of the fancier restaurants in the town one over?" Bo wanted this to be special. And since Travis worked at the diner, Bo thought his man might like the change.

"I wouldn't want to be anywhere else. This is where I met you, made new friends, gained a family and my life back." Travis stopped and wrapped his arms around Bo but held himself away to keep from smushing his chest. "This is the perfect place to celebrate."

Bo had to admit, his lover was right. They walked through the glass doors and listened to the hum of conversations carrying on around them as they found their seats. They slid into a booth, both on the same side, and perused a menu they already had memorized from front to back.

One of the two high school kids Bear had hired to help in the dining room came over with two glasses of water. She took their order, which was the special, roast beef dinner, because Bear was cooking and Bo's partner's favorite meal was roast beef. Anytime now Rick and Josh would be walking through those doors to visit and have dinner. Things like that were what made Brighton special—family, familiarity, the people.

Travis cuddled into Bo's side as they waited for their meal and Bo noticed a new person sitting in a booth in the back corner. He was a big man with curly blond hair and blue eyes, and reminded Bo of someone.

"Love, have you seen that guy before?"

Travis looked up to see where Bo was looking before answering. "Yeah. He got into town this morning before the end of my shift. He's a doctor."

"How do you know that?"

"He has the caduceus on his necklace."

"I'm sorry, what?"

"You know that medical symbol you see. The one with two snakes wrapped around a rod. It's supposed to be the rod wielded by a Greek god of healing and medicine," Travis explained. "When I was going through all my surgeries several of the doctors and nurses had some form of that symbol somewhere, like a necklace, bracelet, or pin. I asked him why he was wearing it."

"You up and asked him?" Bo questioned, knowing how shy Travis was.

"Okay, I got Sarah to ask him. She was already having a conversation with him so I had her throw that in out of curiosity. He's a plastic surgeon, that's all I know."

Bo had no idea why he couldn't let it go but there was something so familiar about the guy. That could be good or bad in his line of work. "I'll be right back, sweetheart. I'll go introduce myself in case he needs anything."

"Sure, in case he needs anything, right." Travis nodded. He knew Bo was going to check the stranger out.

A few people noticed him approach the table where the man was reading what looked like a thick textbook. The spine read "Refurbishing an Old Building." Bo waited until the man noticed him.

"Hello, I'm Bo," he said when the guy looked up. The feeling that he knew this man grew even stronger. Bo held out his hand for him to shake but the stranger stood instead, displaying his bandaged hands. Bo had been so consumed by trying to figure out why he felt he knew the man that he didn't notice the man's hands. "I'm Saint, nice to meet you. Care to join me?"

Bo noticed two other things right off the bat, the man was favoring his right side and he was huge. Taller than Bo's six foot five, and this guy had muscles to spare. The man's eyes read nothing but welcome so Bo thought he'd sit for a moment.

"I wanted to introduce myself, I'm Bo Mason and I'm a police officer here in Brighton. If you need anything, give me a call at the station." Bo smiled hoping he didn't look like a complete busybody.

Saint grinned before saying, "Officer Mason, my name is Dr. Frank Jeffrey but I don't go by that anymore."

"That's okay. I don't need your full name."

Saint smiled even wider. "I'd be disappointed if you didn't take it. My little brother told me Brighton was a close-knit community that looked out for him."

"Your brother?"

"Johnny Jeffrey. He's going to marry, I'm guessing, a relative of yours named Gabe Mason. Please correct me if I'm presuming."

"That's it, that's why I thought I recognized you. You and your brother look alike. Well other than the size difference," Bo muttered. "And yeah, he's marrying my cousin."

At that, Saint laughed, which made the big man hold his side as if trying to ease a pain. Bo could see his and Travis's food being delivered to their table and decided the man wasn't a threat and no he hadn't seen him from one of their mug shots. "Well, I'll leave you in peace. I imagine we'll see you at the wedding." Bo wanted to ask about his injuries but decided that was one step too far.

"If everything works out I intend to be there."

That was an odd thing to say, but Bo let it go, and walked back to his amazing boyfriend who looked at him through hooded eyes. Bo knew exactly what Travis was dreaming about and intended to fill those desires as soon as they got home. For now, he sat beside his lover in a diner full of friends, family, and neighbors, in a town he was proud to call home.

He was a fortunate man.

Chapter Eight

Dr. Frank Jeffrey—Saint

Saint concentrated harder then he'd ever had to before as he tried to get back to his motel room without alerting anyone. He didn't need these people to waste their time worrying about him. He smiled and waved to people as they passed by on the sidewalk and made sure his happy mask was firmly in place at least until he passed the threshold of his motel room. The weather had turned colder, but at least there wasn't any snow to navigate. If he was at his cabin in upstate New York, he'd be shoveling piles of it, not as if he could shovel *shit* now anyway.

He took the last hundred feet at an almost jog, which didn't help his pain, but he'd made it inside with no one the wiser. He tamped down his need to rage and scream at the injustice of it all, but what the hell was the use. Nothing would change. And he'd gotten the best opinions New York's finest doctors could offer.

With the limited mobility he had left in his hands, Saint removed his boots and jeans before sliding his shirt over his head. He looked down at the bandages wrapped around his waist and checked for blood. He'd thought for sure he'd busted a stitch, but there wasn't a red spot to be found.

He picked up his pain medication, which the pharmacist had placed in an easy open container for people with arthritis that Saint wanted to chuck across the room. He wasn't an invalid. Once his tantrum faded he took his time wrapping his fingers around the bottle of water, not wanting to drop it, and swallowed a pill down. He didn't like taking them, but had to admit at times like these they were necessary. The pain became too much to bear.

In the blink of an eye he was transported back to the chilling scene where he was lying in the dirt surrounded by puddles of his blood. He shook his head, pushing that memory deep, where no one would see it.

Using both hands, he set the water bottle down on the bedside table and slowly crawled onto the bed and used his legs to get his body under the covers. It had been nice to hear that he and his brother resembled one another. In the past, everyone had always been overly concerned about their differences. Saint loved his brother more than Johnny knew. That's why he'd done what was necessary to ensure his brother's peace.

Saint looked around his room. His home for the next little while wasn't anything like the typical small-town motel. This place could rival any five-star hotel he'd stayed in. He even had a patio with potted plants and a longue jutting out of the back of his room. The bed was a California king, the room was spotless, the décor upscale, the furniture was newish, and a large flat-screen TV hung on the wall. The room was equipped with a single-serve coffeemaker and a mini-fridge. Waiting on his doorstep this morning, along with his continental basket of fresh baked muffins, croissant, a ramekin of butter, and individual bottles of British jellies, he had two newspapers rolled up standing against the wall next to the door—the small local paper and *The Wall Street Journal*. This place provided superior accommodations for a vacation, even though that was the last thing he was here to do.

His medication began to kick in as his eyes slowly closed. Tomorrow would be another day. A gift he'd almost lost while simultaneously being his own personal hell.

Chapter Nine

Grady and Ben

Ben pulled their new SUV up to the side of the cottage, put it in park, and turned off the ignition. He turned to look at the gorgeous man sleeping soundly in the reclined bucket seat beside him. Grady had worked the night shift before they'd loaded up and headed out, and Ben was reluctant to wake him. However, there was no way he would leave his boyfriend crammed in the seat when spacious beds were only feet away.

"Babe, we're here. Wake up," he whispered, not wanting to startle him.

Grady began to move and stretched his arms above his head before opening his big brown eyes and gazing at Ben. "Hey, we're here already? That was fast."

"No comments about my driving, you were asleep."

"Sure, Andretti." Grady smiled before leaning over for a kiss Ben was happy to give.

The touch of his soft lips never failed to excite Ben, but he held himself in check. Grady needed rest after a long shift protecting Brighton. "Let's get you inside, sweetheart."

"I like the sound of that," Grady playfully growled, pulling Ben in for another kiss. Several moments later both were breathing heavily, and the windows began to fog.

"Come on, you need to get some more rest, there's plenty of time for that later."

Grady frowned, but whatever complaint he was going to level lost its effectiveness when he yawned. Ben laughed and opened the driver's door, walked to the back and retrieved their bags, and headed to the front door behind his drowsy lover. Ben still had the occasional twinge of pain in his shoulder from the gunshot wound he'd sustained, but other than that, he was back to full strength.

The Mason family's light blue cottage stood with its wood shutters closed and door locked tight. No one had been here since his mom and aunts had come up to set everything to right after the mess with Grady's father. Ben had brought along new bedding, food, drinks, and whatever else they might need for their little getaway.

Ben noticed Grady pause before putting the key into the lock on the door. There were a lot of not-so-happy memories here, and Ben hoped they had made the right decision to create new memories.

Grady squared his shoulders and turned to look at Ben. "Are you okay with all of this?"

Ben should have known that while he was worried how this would affect Grady, his man would do the same for him. Ben set their bags down and took his amazing man into his arms.

"I want us to be able to come here. I've always loved this place." Ben had enjoyed staying at the lake as often as possible, and he refused to let some asshole take that away from him.

Grady looked at him for a few seconds, nodded, and turned to unlock the door. Of course, it opened with a squeal of disuse, and the interior was dark. However, as soon as he had a chance, he'd open the shutters and let the light and fresh air flow in. He and Grady took their bedding and bags to one of the bedrooms before bringing in the cooler of food. Ben insisted they head back into the bedroom and make the bed. He knew Grady was going to crash soon.

Sure enough, ten minutes after they'd gotten the bedroom squared away, Grady was fading fast. He was fighting to keep his eyes open. "Go to sleep," Ben ordered. "I can take care of everything and I'll wake you for supper."

"I can't leave you to do everything by yourself, babe."

"You're not leaving me to do anything. I'm telling you to go get some rest because I intend to take advantage of being out in the middle of nowhere. Once the room airs out, I'm gonna get this fire started, and then I'll declare this a clothes-free cottage."

Grady's eyes turned fiery as he reached out for Ben, only to come up empty when he backed away. "Sleep now, play later, love. That's the deal."

"You drive a hard bargain, babe. But okay, I'll go get some shut-eye but if you need anything you wake me up."

It felt wonderful to have a partner to share everything, especially the responsibilities. Typically, Ben had always been the one to provide everything and take responsibility for the same. The big, muscled firefighter. Now, it wasn't all on him.

"I will wake you if necessary," he promised. *Never going to happen.*

Grady shook his head as if he'd read Ben's mind but acquiesced before giving him a kiss and walking to their bedroom. Once he heard the door close Ben went to work. He planned to have this place comfy-cozy by the time Grady woke up. Ben wanted them to have good memories here in one of his favorite places.

He understood that Grady's first impression of the cottage had been skewed by the former threat of a stalker hovering over them. When the stalker turned out to be Grady's father, it was a shock, and Ben wasn't sure if his lover had fully recovered. But for the next three days it would be love and laughter that filled their time here, not fear or pain. They'd be back to Brighton a couple days before Gabe and Johnny's wedding. Ben would never miss his cousin and fellow firefighter's big day.

One by one, he opened the old wooden shutters as he'd done hundreds of times before. The cottage immediately filled with light, dispelling any trace of gloom. He opened a couple of windows, then went to the back of the house, or the front as some people called it because of its aspect. He stopped to look out onto the quiet lake. Birds took flight from the surface, leaving trails in the water after they were long gone. Tall trees stood guard around the cottage, but most of the flowers had gone with the cooler weather.

It was an honor to be allowed to stand among this beauty. Trees hundreds of years old a constant reminder of how fleeting his time was on earth. After everything he'd gone through and how close he'd come to death, it was even more poignant.

Ben shook himself, freeing the melancholy feelings that kept trying to cling to him. His brush with death reinforced his need to live life to the fullest, and he intended to do just that. He went back to work on the shutters, closed the windows, and then turned on the electricity and the water from the well. They had everything they needed right here, and family and friends knew not to call unless it was an emergency. This was their private time and he didn't want anything or anyone to mess with it.

Life had been hectic since he'd been released from the hospital for the second time. Between doctors and physio appointments, moving Grady into their home, searching for and finding Grady's brother Randy, work and recovery... time had been rushing by and neither of them had had a chance to celebrate their union, and simply enjoy the moment, until now.

Ben brought five loads of dried wood into the cottage and set it in the bin near the large stone fireplace. On either side of the fireplace were garden doors leading out to the patio overlooking the water. He had special plans for the spot on the rug in front of the roaring fire he was busy building. Everything would be ready for him to lavish love and attention onto the man who meant everything to him.

***

Grady arched his back, desperate to feel the work-roughened hands of his lover as they ghosted over his chest. He hadn't opened his eyes yet, basking in the loving attention he was receiving from Ben.

"Open your eyes, love, dinner is almost ready. There's enough time for you to have a shower and join me in the living room," Ben whispered in Grady's ear. The deep timbre of Ben's voice seemed to vibrate through Grady's suddenly overheated body.

He opened his eyes to find the man of his dreams sitting beside him on the bed wearing a dark blue bathrobe. His hair was wet from what Grady presumed was Ben's shower.

"Why didn't you wait for me? We could have taken a shower together." Grady tried for his best pout but by the smile on Ben's face, it wasn't working.

"If I had done that, dinner would have been ruined by the time we made it out of this room. Now, get up and put this on after your shower." Ben held up another robe identical to his own. "This is the only piece of clothing we wear while inside the cottage."

Oh hell yes, things were looking up. Grady reached for the robe, imagining all the fun to be had in wearing only that. At the last moment, Ben swooped in and pulled Grady into his arms before taking Grady's mouth in an all-consuming kiss. By the time Ben released him, Grady had been well and truly snogged. His heart was racing and his dick was hard.

"Don't take too long, babe," Ben told him as he stood and walked out of the room with a noticeable tent in the front of his robe.

Grady wasted no time in jumping into the shower, his man was waiting for him one room away. He was surprised by how relaxed he felt while being back in the place where he'd almost lost Ben. Initially, Grady wasn't certain about coming back to this place, but he realized how much the cottage meant to Ben and there was no way Grady would keep him from it. However, everywhere Grady looked he was reminded of what his father had tried to do to the man Grady loved.

He showered quickly, shaved, and donned his robe, ready for the evening alone with Ben. It felt as though they'd been constantly moving since they'd first met and had never had the chance to enjoy one another. Now was that time.

Grady walked out the bedroom door and down the short hallway on his way to the main room. He wasn't prepared for what he found waiting for him. All the windows were now uncovered and a stunning sunset could be seen dipping into the lake. A fire roared in the hearth, and the coffee table had been removed and in its place were plush-looking blankets and pillows surrounding what appeared to be a short stump, but without the bark. It was, in essence, a nest. The main overhead lights had been turned off, leaving the fire to paint everything in its golden glow.

Ben came from the kitchen area carrying two plates. "There you are. Right on time, babe."

Grady couldn't help but smile wide. Ben had done all this for him. He joined Ben in the center of their blanket-buffeted nest and helped Ben set the plates down beside a dented silver bucket full of ice chilling a bottle of wine. Grady took the opportunity to pull Ben into his arms and held him tight.

"Thank you, babe."

Ben cupped Grady's cheek and murmured, "Anything for you." Ben's soft lips felt like heaven against Grady's skin as his lover kissed the side of his neck. "I've been waiting for this all day. Naked time."

Grady reached for his belt holding his robe closed as Ben did the same. Inch by inch, Ben's tanned skin revealed itself to Grady's appreciative gaze. Neither looked away from the other, enjoying the freedom they had being here together. Both lowered to the floor after a few explorative caresses and Grady looked at his plate sitting on one side of the wide piece of wood of the stump. He knew he shouldn't be surprised about finding his favorite meal of lasagna on the menu, but the care Ben had taken to prepare all this was humbling. Grady was a lucky man.

"Everything is perfect." Grady voice cracked slightly. "I love you so much."

Ben took Grady's hand and kissed his palm. "I love you just as much."

Sometimes Grady thought all this was too good to be true, but then he remembered what they'd been through to be together and knew it was real. He dug into his meal, moaning as the sweet tomatoes, gooey cheese, and perfectly cooked noodles hit his tongue. This was heaven. Sitting in the glow of the fireplace eating an amazing meal with the sexiest man he'd ever seen was the stuff dreams were made of. Ben poured two glasses of wine before digging into his own plate of food with a moan of his own.

"You made all this while I was sleeping?" Grady asked, duly impressed.

"Well, I prepared a lot of it ahead of time while you were on shift last night. The rest I did when we got here. Do you like it?"

"Oh babe, it's phenomenal. All the more special because you made it for me."

Ben smiled, making Grady's heart skip a beat at how breathtaking his partner was. It wasn't simply his appearance, though that would be godlike stature; it was the whole package. Ben's bravery, compassion, strength, love, and kindness rounded out the total picture of Grady's man.

They continued eating with the occasional touch or caress, and by the end of the meal, their legs were intertwined to one side of the stump they were using as a table. Ben took Grady's empty plate, untangled himself before standing, and deposited the dishes in the sink. Grady watched Ben's beautiful ass flex as he walked away, but the return journey held him mesmerized. He could feel his own cock hardening by the second.

"Before dessert I have something for you," Ben announced as he sat down and reached between the couch cushions to retrieve a long slender box.

Grady didn't know what to say. Ben had made this evening so memorable to begin with he had no idea what else there could be. Ben held the box out and Grady's hand shook as he took it. His love remained quiet as Grady unwrapped the bow around the box and opened it. What he found inside made him gasp.

The gold shined in the firelight as he pulled the necklace from the box. The chain wasn't overly thick, but was substantial enough he wouldn't worry wearing it. On the end was a small medallion with the image of Saint Michael the Archangel, the patron saint of police officers. It was more than decorative and beautiful—it had strong meaning.

"I know we haven't talked about religion before, and I hope this doesn't upset you, but I had Father John bless it before I brought it here." Ben blushed but continued, "I figured it couldn't hurt to have the big guy on our side. Now, when I'm not with you I feel a bit better knowing that someone's looking out for you." Ben looked away.

Grady would have none of that. There was no reason for his partner to be embarrassed. This was the most significant and stunning gift he'd ever received. He lifted the stump and placed it off to the side before crawling over to his lover.

He cupped Ben's cheek and said with a slight tremble in his voice, "Thank you. No one has ever given me something this special. I'll treasure it forever." Grady held out the necklace. "Will you put it on me?"

Ben took the necklace before motioning for Grady to turn around. He complied and moments later felt the chain lying against his skin. He looked down at the medallion that now sat in the center of his chest and traced it with his fingertip.

Strong arms wrapped around him from behind. "I'll do anything to keep you safe. I want to spend the rest of my life with you."

Had he ever been loved so thoroughly? Grady leaned back onto Ben's chest and soaked in the love and care his partner was lavishing on him. Ben's hands roamed over Grady's chest, making his nipples harden before pinching them between his fingers and sending a jolt of need straight to his hardening cock. The groan that escaped his lips seemed to bounce off the walls in the quiet room.

"Make love to me, Ben." Grady didn't want to wait another minute. He craved his lover who was currently kissing his ear. Ben brought every need Grady had storming to the surface, begging to be satisfied.

"Oh, I will, but I want to love on you for a while first," Ben purred, his voice like warm honey flowing over Grady's hot skin. With every lick and suck, goose bumps appeared and excitement surged through his veins.

Ben lowered Grady to the soft blankets covering the floor and began mapping Grady's body with his hot, wet tongue. His breathing sped up as his lover explored every inch. The one time he tried to reach for Ben, his hands were caught and placed above his head.

"I want this to be all about you, sweetheart," Ben explained before taking Grady's cock in his mouth and swallowing him down his throat.

Grady cried out at the sudden intense pleasure flooding through him. Ben played his body like a finely tuned instrument, bringing him close to the edge before backing off, never allowing him to fall over. By the time Ben slid his finger into him, Grady was trembling with need. One quickly became two, then three. It seemed as though Ben needed him as much as Grady wanted Ben.

"Ready, babe?" Ben asked as he lined himself up with Grady's hole.

"More than ready. I need you inside me."

The slight burn was quickly replaced with desire as Ben brushed against his prostate, sending Grady flying. By the time Ben was fully seated inside him, Grady was a panting, moaning mess begging for more. Ben was the only man with this much power over him. But, no matter how lost he became in the throes of passion, Ben was there to guide him home. It was freeing being able to completely let go without fear.

His world narrowed to the sensations running through his body and Ben's hooded green eyes. Soon he felt his balls pull up tight and the pressure building and knew he'd not be able to stop this time.

"Ben, I'm…" His voice was lost as his orgasm overtook him. Pulse after pulse was pulled from his body until he had nothing left to give.

Ben's roar filled the room moments before he collapsed onto Grady. It was a good thing they were the same size so that he could hold Ben's weight. He ran his hands over Ben's sweaty skin, tracing his muscles as well as the scar left behind by Grady's father's bullet.

"Love you," Ben said, and kissed Grady gently before rolling onto his side. "You're everything to me, babe."

Grady held him tight and after a couple minutes, Ben began to snore. Considering everything he'd done today, driving up here, and preparing all this for Grady, he understood completely. He reached over and pulled a blanket over the two of them. The fire was still going strong as he took a good look around the room.

Before today, he would have not seen the appeal to a place that held so many bad memories. Now, looking at the thick timbers, mismatched rugs, old family photos covering every wall, and fishing trophies that sat proudly on the mantel, Grady could see the draw. Ben's love of the place made Grady look at it through different eyes, ones that did not include his father.

He reached for his medallion and held it between his fingers. This was what love was meant to be. This was the all-encompassing feeling he never thought he'd have, and the man he never dreamed he'd be fortunate enough to be loved by.

He looked down at the engraving of Saint Michael and smiled. Every bad memory he'd had in this cottage was being replaced with love. Now, as Ben had wished, this cottage had transformed back into a place the two of them could escape to as often as possible. Ben had given him this peace and Grady loved him for it.

Now he had to wait for round two as he looked at the tasty man lying on his chest. With this level of temptation, Grady definitely needed the patience of a saint.

Chapter Ten

The White Hair Crew

Rose, Jackie, Betty, Bertha, and Joan, grandmas all, watched as the latest arrival in town walked down Main Street on his way from the Brighton Motel. His name was Saint, and according to the Brighton grapevine, he was Johnny's brother. Which made sense considering the wedding coming up. However, Rose recognized a lost soul when she saw one.

"So what's the plan?" Joan asked.

"What do you mean?" Rose asked, knowing full well the other four already knew who she was thinking about.

"Really, we're way too old to play that game, Rose." Bertha laughed as she stirred her cup of wild berry tea. "Out with it."

"Do any of you get the feeling that Dr. Saint Jeffrey is struggling?" she asked.

"He looks like he's been through something awful. There is so much pain in his eyes and it's not all the physical kind. Although that boy does look like he's been hurt, with those bandages and all," Jackie stated.

"The question is, what are we going to do about it, ladies?" Betty asked as she pulled a notepad from her bedazzled purse. Her granddaughter had made it for her as a birthday gift and she never went anywhere without it.

Rose thought about it for a moment before asking, "He's here for Johnny's wedding, right?"

"Yep, that's what Travis said," Bertha told them.

"So we have ten days to figure it out. I say we start by getting to know him, and that can start right now," Rose said as she motioned toward the front doors of the diner. Saint was walking in with the same book he carried under his arm everywhere she'd seen him.

Joan stood and called out, "Saint. Come sit with us, young man." Mrs. Walker wasn't known for her subtlety.

Saint looked ready to bolt but Rose had to give him credit, he squared his shoulders and walked over to their table. "Good morning, ladies."

"Good morning, Saint," the Crew said in unison, and the man took a half step back.

"Yep, we're giving off the cult vibe, girls, and scaring the poor young man. Tone it down a touch," Rose admonished before pulling an extra chair over from the next table and motioning for him to sit. "Join us for a coffee, Dr. Jeffrey." It wasn't a question.

"Saint. I don't go by doctor any longer," he explained a bit gruffly. "I'm sorry but I won't be able to join you ladies, my brother wanted to meet me for coffee."

"That's fine, young man, we'll keep you company until Johnny arrives," Jackie said as she waved down Katie, one of the high school girls who was waitressing. Rose would have to thank her for her quick thinking later.

"I hope Johnny brings Lucy with him. She's such a sweet child and she's starting to come out of her shell. But she still won't go to anyone other than Gabe and Johnny," Betty commented before stuffing her knitting back into her patchwork bag.

Saint scanned the diner as if looking for a way out. When he saw none his shoulders drooped and he sat. "How are you ladies this morning?" She and the other women knew the poor man wanted to be anywhere other than here, but at least he was polite.

For the next five minutes, the Crew chatted about various aches and pains each woke up with as Rose watched him navigate his coffee with the palms of both bandaged hands. It reminded her of how boxers tape their hands before putting boxing gloves on. The more the women talked the calmer Saint became until he began leaning back in his chair, releasing some of the anxiety he was carrying around. Rose imagined him to be quite a nice fellow if he weren't carrying around so much sorrow.

"So, are you going to be buying a place here in Brighton to refurbish?" Rose asked while pointing to the big book he'd been hauling around since arriving.

Saint ran his finger across the spine before answering. "No ma'am, I'm not buying in Brighton. I have a place in LA that I'll be heading to after the wedding."

"Los Angeles, how exciting," Bertha said while waving her right hand and almost knocking Rose in the face if she hadn't ducked. Saint smiled but it quickly melted away.

"I don't know about exciting, but from what I've heard and seen, it's going to take a lot of work bringing the building back to its former glory."

"Do you have a contractor set up yet?" Rose asked, her mind already working.

"No. I haven't found the right person for the job. I need someone who has extensive knowledge about refurbishing old buildings in DTLA, and has contacts in the city. The permitting process is a nightmare." Well, that question had gotten him in high dungeon.

"Now, don't you worry," Rose told him, "my nephew's son is a contractor out that way. I'll give him a call and see if he can recommend someone."

"Kind of you. But I'm...picky. I couldn't ask you to put yourself out," Saint said with a fair amount of starch in his voice.

"You didn't ask, I offered. This is Brighton after all." Rose patted his arm and waved away any further discussion even though she could tell he wasn't cottoning to the suggestion one bit.

Saint looked ready to continue arguing the point, but a loud gasp had them all turning their heads to find Johnny with Gabe, who was holding Lucy, a few feet away from their table.

"Frank, my god, what happened to your hands?"

Simultaneously, Lucy squirmed to get out of Gabe's arms and ran to a man who should have been a stranger yelling, "Saint, Saint."

Chapter Eleven

Saint

Saint was stunned as Lucy bounced up and down beside his chair, looking so much happier than the last time they'd been together. The table had fallen silent, and both his brother and the guy he assumed was Gabe stared at him and Lucy as if they had four heads. He knew explanations would be expected, but he didn't know if he was up to reliving the entire nightmare for public consumption.

"Perhaps we should discuss this someplace else," Saint suggested. Even though the situation sucked, he couldn't help the genuine smile on his face at seeing his younger brother after such a long time.

The shock in Johnny's eyes faded to concern. Saint could no longer keep Lucy at bay and picked her up onto his lap with the unmistakable hiss of pain.

"Where else are you hurt?" Johnny asked, but thankfully, the man with his brother stepped in.

"Sweetheart, we should take your brother to the house where he'd be more comfortable."

Saint found that a bit forward considering he hadn't been invited to their home before. They'd wanted to meet him here at the diner, and who could blame them, he was essentially a stranger now.

Johnny seemed to snap out of it and looked around the diner. "Absolutely. Of course. You can come with us and we'll bring you back to the motel later. Do you need any help standing?"

Throughout this, Lucy sat as happy as a clam on his lap. Saint was positive the entire diner was wondering how a plastic surgeon from New York knew an orphaned toddler from Costa Rica.

That question opened a Pandora's box he'd fought to keep closed for many years. Nevertheless, with the complete joy only a child could give, the box had been blown wide open leaving him without protection to face his brother, whom he hadn't spoken to in years.

Chapter Twelve

Vincent and Tristan

Tristan opened the box that had been delivered to the main house that morning, excited to be able to get his hands on the hard copies. Packing paper went flying into the air as he dug to get to his prize, and there it was, all shiny and new, *Protected*, the first novel from his new series. It followed the lives of a group of military men finding their way after getting out of the service. *Yeah, yeah, where would I come up with that idea?*

The words of his grade eight English teacher floated through his head: write what you know. After everything he'd seen and been through, Tristan had a wealth of information to call upon. He took one book out before setting the box on the kitchen floor, and then he reached for his mug of coffee. Sitting at the large table, his hand on his book, his gaze was drawn to the wall mosaic that his lover had made for him out of his grandmother's smashed dishes. That gift spoke volumes. He remembered the pain he had felt when he'd learned the china had been smashed, that the last physical remnant of his beloved grans had been destroyed. But Vincent had put everything to rights by creating this incredible mosaic.

Luna came running in through her doggie-door followed by two of her puppies. Tristan couldn't believe how much time had flown by—the pups were old enough to roam on their own and freely moved between the main house and Tristan and Vincent's home.

"Hello, pretty girl. What are you all up to today?" Tristan asked as Luna and her pups jumped onto the couch and got comfortable. "Ah, I see, nap time."

The Sentinels had gotten a routine of sorts down since the puppies came along and Tristan was sharing visitation rights with Sam. The doggie family went where they pleased, begging treats and spreading love wherever they went. Soon though one of those balls of fluff would be leaving them behind to start a new life with a different owner.

If he'd thought the Sentinels were protective of their family and friends, he'd marveled at their downright obsession over a defenseless puppy. Before they would consider letting one of their doggie family go, the adopters had to fill out a detailed, and rather intrusive, questionnaire, which Shannon and Matthew would dissect. Then there was a home visit to make sure the puppy would be safe and cared for. Last was the contract that allowed the team members to retrieve the puppy if they felt it was in danger.

The first female puppy was going to Gabe and Johnny's adopted daughter, Lucy. Yep, they had to go through all the steps. Tristan smiled remembering the day the whole team showed up at Gabe and Johnny's house for inspection. Apparently, the whole time the Sentinels clomped through the house and yard, Johnny watched them, looking nervous, while Gabe sat back watching a princess movie with Lucy. By the end of the "home inspection," the whole team had ended up on the couch or floor watching the movie right along with them.

Family. You had to love 'em.

Speaking of family, Tristan's mom and dad came down for a visit to meet everyone and scolded him for not telling them about his Lyme infection. Somehow, the fact that he didn't want to worry them wasn't a good enough reason. Vincent couldn't contain his "told ya so" and sat back to watch the fireworks. Eventually they'd calmed down and were happy Tristan was on the mend. Lord knows what they would have done if they ever found out about his ex and his stalker.

Tristan lifted his right hand and flexed the fingers out before bringing them in to make a fist. His thumb and little finger did as he wanted but the other three could make it only halfway. He'd been in physiotherapy for months, but recovery was slow and his joints still ached. Funny how having to fight for his own and Sam's lives put a completely new spin on things. His damaged hand wasn't that much of an issue in the grand scheme of things.

Working through his issues with Dr. Gordon had been amazing so far. Now Tristan understood why everyone had recommended the doc so highly. Tristan was still processing his guilt over killing Ryan

Graham, but at least it no longer felt as though he was suffocating when he thought of it.

Vincent had been gone for two days and wasn't due back for another. Though they were essentially on their holiday vacation, a call had come in from an old friend who needed his help. Vincent and his friend were protecting a man scheduled to testify against two members of the Sorrel crime family in Chicago.

Though Tristan missed Vincent, he understood that this was a part of his life, and it was his calling. Vincent had fought to protect people his entire life, through his military service and as a member of the Sentinel team. Tristan would never do anything to stop him from following his calling, even if he missed him like crazy.

Tristan walked out onto his front porch with his coffee and sat on the pillow-covered swing that faced the gently flowing river running beside their house. They'd chosen this spot to make their home. This was their idea of paradise.

The box of Christmas decoration his parents had sent was waiting patiently by the fireplace alongside the ones Vincent's parents had given them when they had visited them in Arizona. Both boxes held new ornaments, some handmade, and a few heirloom pieces. Before Vincent had left, he and Tristan had gone to the local garden center and picked out a small loblolly pine tree. It was still in its own pot, and after Christmas, they intended to plant it somewhere on their property.

Everything was sitting, waiting, ready to go for when the man who owned Tristan's heart came home.

Tristan pushed his foot against the wood decking and sent the porch swing into motion. Even though the wind had turned a bit colder these past couple of days, he still loved to sit on the porch. Besides, the new sweater Mrs. Walker had made for him kept him nice and toasty. It was bright red to match his hair, and Tristan loved it.

He was busy getting his laptop set up when he heard an engine. He wondered if one of the guys was coming out for another visit. Tristan, Matthew, Sam, and Randy had become each other's support group when any of their men were away on assignments. It helped make the time more bearable, and they enjoyed each other's company.

Concerned, he noted this engine sounded more powerful than his friends' ATVs. He set his laptop down and stood looking toward the spot where their laneway broke through the tree line. The moment he saw it, his heart started pounding in his throat. Vincent was home.

Tristan jumped off the porch and ran toward their garage as Vincent parked his big truck beside Tristan's new feisty Fiesta, in hot pepper metallic red.

Tristan didn't stop running until he jumped into Vincent's open arms. The feel of those strong arms wrapping around his body gave Tristan a peace he felt only when his partner was near.

"I've missed you, sparrow," Vincent groaned as he crushed Tristan to his muscled chest.

"Same here, babe." Tristan's voice was muffled by Vincent's shirt.

The two stood in the driveway for several minutes, neither seemed able to let go of the other. Funny how everything felt as though it was in its right place when they were together.

"You weren't due back for another day. What happened? Was anyone hurt?" Tristan asked before pulling away to get a good look at his man. "I told you not to come back with a scratch." His lover knew he was joking…sort of.

"No, sparrow, I'm not hurt. As it turns out, the two Sorrel crime bosses he was set to testify against turned up dead," Vincent explained. "So since there wasn't a trial, the witness was sent off to his new life in the witness protection program." He lowered his head to take Tristan's lips in a hungry kiss.

Vincent bent and then picked up Tristan, pulling him into that massive chest, and headed for the house. Tristan was on the same page. He needed to be as close to his lover as he could get and that required a lot less clothing.

For someone who thought he'd never know what real love felt like, Tristan was making up for lost time.

***

Vincent stirred the cream into his coffee, grabbed the two mugs, and headed for the living room. The main lights had been dimmed, and the Christmas lights were glowing, making the living room feel cozy. It was a stark difference to his last two days stuck in a cheap hotel in downtown Chicago. The Windy City was way too crowded for his liking. He looked out their front window at the stars hanging low in the sky. This was his idea of heaven, and his angel was currently sitting in front of their first Christmas tree wearing only his boxers, waiting for him.

"Here you go, sparrow," Vincent said as he handed over one of the mugs before sitting down beside Tristan on the floor.

"Thank you." His beauty's smile never ceased to make Vincent's heart skip a beat. His old life couldn't compare to this and the love they shared. "I've been dying to go through these boxes."

Vincent sat back and watched as one by one, Tristan removed and unwrapped ornament after ornament. His face aglow as each was revealed, as if each was a Christmas gift on their own.

"I made this in second grade," he announced while holding up a colorful clay handprint. It had sparkles and feathers glued all along the edges. "I had style even back then."

Vincent couldn't help but laugh and pulled his love even closer. After a quick kiss, Tristan continued to sort through all the ornaments when he held up one of Vincent's, looking confused.

Vincent raised a brow. "It was supposed to be a horse from our ranch." He shrugged at the lump. "I was five."

Tristan tilted his chin down, doing a poor job of concealing his grin. "It's adorable." He reached into the box and grabbed another item. "Oh my god, is this your cowboy hat?"

Sure enough, he pulled out a pint-size straw Stetson from the box. It had been Vincent's first. "I didn't even know my mom had saved this."

Tristan reached up and placed it on his head. Vincent was sure that the brim that hadn't even fit his small head as a child was no more than the size of a small saucer now. But it brought back fond memories. New memories with the man with whom he'd spend the rest of his life was Vincent's mission.

"I can imagine you running wild with the ranch as your playground. Sounds like paradise," Tristan said wistfully.

Vincent gathered his sparrow close. "It was. I've been fortunate to have had a wonderful childhood, but nothing compares to my life now, with you."

Tristan wrapped his arms around Vincent's neck. "You sweet talker, you. Keep that up and I just might keep you."

"Might keep me, huh?" Vincent began tickling his sassy boyfriend's sides until he was out of breath from laughing so much. "You're stuck with me, brat."

"I'm completely on board with that," Tristan said once he could breathe properly again.

Vincent pulled over the box Tristan's parents had given them and pulled out a Santa covered in various shades of blue.

"That was my blue phase," Tristan answered without skipping a beat.

His sparrow, an original, and all his.

Vincent remembered the moment he first laid eyes on Tristan at the Brighton Police Station. Tristan had stood ready to defend his friend Grady that day, not concerned in the least that he was the smallest person in the room. His curly fire-red hair was messed from running his fingers through it, and Tristan's striking green eyes caught Vincent's attention within seconds of entering the room. He hadn't been able to look away since. Nor did he wish to.

The rest of the evening played out with nostalgia and laughter. Old memories relived and new memories made. By the end of the night they sat together on the floor, Tristan leaning back against Vincent's chest, both admiring the fully decorated tree with a child's cowboy hat as its star.

Tristan had added light to Vincent's life much like the Christmas tree they were sitting beside. Tristan was Vincent's light, leading him home after each mission, after every time he risked his life to save a life, and he knew he was blessed to have it.

This complete joy he never saw coming would be his greatest gift this year, and for many more to come.

Chapter Thirteen

Gabe and Johnny

Johnny helped his brother out of the truck and onto the walkway leading to their home. Gabe held a sleeping Lucy close to his chest, and headed for her bedroom to lay her down for her nap. Saint looked ashen and weak. Nothing like what Johnny remembered of his brother's movie-star good looks. He was still huge but it seemed as if the life had been drained out of him, painfully.

"Do you want anything to eat or drink, Saint?" Johnny asked as he helped him sit in one of the chairs in the living room.

'Yes, water, please," he replied in the same monotone voice Johnny had noted he'd used when they spoke at the diner.

Saint's eyes were another story. Flat and void of emotion, the only time Johnny saw any happiness there was when his brother looked at him.

Johnny left the living room quickly, eager to get back to his brother as fast as possible. By the time he pulled a bottle of water from the fridge, Gabe was at his side in the kitchen.

He pulled Johnny into a much-needed hug and said, "Don't worry, we'll find out what happened to him."

"No matter what, he's still my brother. If he's in trouble, we have to help him," Johnny stated firmly. It didn't matter that he hadn't seen him in years, Saint was his brother.

"We will figure it out, I promise."

Together they walked back into the living room to find Saint in exactly the same position, as if he was afraid to move. "Here you go," Johnny said as he handed over the bottle of water.

Saint smiled but remained silent. By the time, they sat down on the opposite couch, Johnny's mind was a jumble of questions but thankfully, Gabe took over.

"Can you tell us what happened to you and how you know our daughter?" Gabe cut to the big questions first.

Saint reached into his jacket pocket and pulled out a prescription bottle, but couldn't manage to open it. Stubbornly, he continued to try until Johnny stood and took the bottle and opened it for him.

"Thank you," Saint huffed out in defeat as Gabe opened his bottle of water as well.

"When I first came here, Gabe had to do those same things for me because my hands were burned," Johnny said while holding up his scarred hands. He'd already explained to his brother what had happened over the phone.

Saint looked at them closely before saying, "I'm glad they're healed nicely and that you had someone there for you. I'm sorry that it wasn't me."

That statement shocked Johnny considering he hadn't heard a peep from his brother in years, but he let it go. The man was in enough pain. He watched as Saint took his pill and shoved the bottle back into his pocket.

"If something's wrong or someone's after you, we can help," Gabe spoke up. "But you need to tell us everything first."

Saint looked at Johnny and Gabe. "I guess I should start at the beginning. I'll do my best to filter it down to the 'highlights.'" There was anger and frustration in his voice, but he sat a bit straighter. "I'm sorry I was such an asshole brother to you the past several years."

"You weren't an asshole. You stopped talking to me, and I never knew why," Johnny replied at the same time Gabe wrapped his arm around him in support. "It hurt not having you in my life."

"I'm sorry," Saint stated. He sounded genuine but Johnny could be hoping he was without knowing. "You were picking out your major for college and Dad was all over you to choose something in the medical field. We both knew that wasn't your calling, but the old man was relentless."

"I remember it was hell, and you were already away at school for a couple years by then."

"Yeah, I was aiming to be a general practitioner. I loved it. The thought of having a small practice of my own. However, Father didn't think it was prestigious enough. Big shock, huh, little brother?"

Johnny couldn't help but smile at "little brother." He'd missed that.

"By then Mom had died and Dad seemed to be on a mission to erase her from our lives. I was home one weekend from school and he was particularly cruel to you."

"I remember. It was the last weekend you ever came home." Johnny knew the date well.

"Yeah, that was the day I signed my deal with the devil," Saint admitted, and Gabe held Johnny closer. "I'd had enough. I couldn't tolerate the way he was treating you, and I told him as much when I cornered him in his study."

"You told him that. What did he do?" Johnny knew his father could be violent when provoked.

"I expected him to flip like he always did. Maybe knock me into the wall again, but he had something more heinous in mind. You know, it wasn't until that day that I realized how evil and manipulative he could be."

Chapter Fourteen

Saint

He felt the chill run through his body exactly as it had that day years ago. He didn't want to have this conversation, but Johnny deserved the truth and to know the danger their father could pose. "Now that I look back on it, I realize the bastard had it all planned out. I'm convinced he'd upped the abuse that weekend for my benefit."

"For your benefit? I was the one who'd been threatened with the possibility of no college. Even though Mom left us enough money to attend, the old man had hold of the strings. If I didn't change my major, he'd not release a cent."

"You're right. He wouldn't have, and mine as well. It was his endgame of sorts. Neither one of us were doing what he wanted, and without Mom there to rein him in, he did whatever he wanted." Memories of that evening flooded back, and Saint felt the same anger, fear, and helplessness he had all those years ago. "I was a college kid, not a strategic general. When I confronted him, I gave him his chance to strike. He'd had the damned contract written up, all ready for my signature."

Johnny looked at his brother, even more confused, and Saint understood this would be a lot to take in. Saint pulled two items from his pocket that were tucked behind the medicine bottle and set them on the coffee table. One was a few old pieces of paper stapled together. The other was a key.

"The contract." Saint nodded at the papers while trying to point with his bandaged hand. "It's kind of surreal that those few pieces of paper could destroy so much."

Gabe reached across the table and picked them up. "How old were you when you signed these?" he asked.

"Over eighteen. Old enough for the contract to be legal. The choice he gave me was clear and exacting. If I didn't sign, both of us would have been left without an education or a future."

"What did the contract say?" Johnny asked.

Saint leaned back in his chair. The pain was finally easing, but he was getting tired. He'd have to rest soon, but not until this was all out in the open. He looked over at Gabe, who had the contract in his hand. "Would you mind reading out the main points for me please, Gabe."

Gabe nodded his agreement and began where all great tragedies began, with shock and doubt. "This can't be legal."

"Oh I assure you it is, even though I was forced to sign it. Which, I learned later, was coercion and would have voided the agreement. I didn't know that then. But that wasn't the reason I adhered to it," Saint explained, giving Gabe a moment to figure it out.

"I understand." Gabe nodded

"You understand what?" Johnny insisted.

"First item agreed upon was that you would change your major to plastic surgery," Gabe began.

"Just like dear old Dad," Saint sighed and sank deeper into the comfortable chair.

"You would complete your education and join your father's practice. You were to cease all contact with Johnny from that day forward. Your father agreed to not encumber or prevent Johnny from completing his marketing degree. He would ensure Johnny received all the money his mother bequeathed to him. But you wouldn't go along with any of it unless he never insinuated himself into Johnny's life or attempted to intimidate him in any way." Gabe looked up. "The last part must have been penned in after the original agreement was typed up. I see it was initialed by both of you."

"I wouldn't allow him to continue to terrorize Johnny. I had to make sure he would stick to the deal so I wrote it in," Shadow explained as he laid his head back against the soft cushions. "With his inheritance, he could do what he wanted. He was free." His voice sounded as groggy as he felt.

He must have drifted off because somehow his body was going back. He realized Johnny was pulling the chair out into a recliner. A moment later a blanket was being tucked in around him.

He was too tired to care that he wasn't done with his story, but Saint needed Johnny to be prepared. He didn't know if or when the danger would come.

Chapter Fifteen

Gabe and Johnny

"Careful if Dad turns up," were the last words Saint muttered before he fell into a deep sleep.

Gabe held Johnny tight. Neither of them had expected what they had learned today.

Initially, when he'd heard Saint was coming to the wedding, Gabe had believed Saint wanted something from Johnny. Hell, he still could, but Gabe wasn't so sure of that any longer. He led his soon-to-be husband to the kitchen so they could talk without disturbing Saint.

They sat at the kitchen island and Johnny took the contract out of Gabe's hands. "Could this be fake?"

"Sure, it could. Anything could be faked given today's technology."

Johnny looked at him closely. "But you don't think it is."

"It doesn't matter what I think, sweetheart."

"Please."

"No. I don't believe it's fake." He had to be honest, even if it hurt. This was a deep, dark family secret that had needed to see the light of day years ago. "But we still don't know how he knows Lucy. I can guess he was her surgeon, but there's a lot of missing information that we'll have to wait to learn. Your brother needs to recuperate from whatever was done to him. I'm surprised he made it to Brighton given his condition."

Johnny shook his head. "I remember that weekend so well. I tried to stay off Dad's radar because he was in a horrible mood. Saint had come home from school and everything seemed normal between us. Then the next morning he was gone without a word and I never spoke to him again other than in passing. I thought he didn't have time for me anymore because he was too busy following in our dad's footsteps. Shit, how did I not suspect something was up? I was wrapped up in my own world and didn't even stop to consider that this wasn't the way my brother behaved. Selfish of me not to have seen that."

"You were young, and you didn't have anyone to help you. The blame lies with your father alone." Gabe tried to ease Johnny's growing guilt. If this turned out to be a scam, Gabe swore Saint would be even more damaged before he left Brighton for putting Johnny through this.

There was a knock on their front door and Gabe stood, gave Johnny a kiss, and went to answer it. He opened the door to find Vincent with a box in his hand, and his lover Tristan waiting on the other side. Gabe brought his finger up to his mouth and made a barely there "shush."

"We brought some of the pup's toys over and her bed so that you can be all ready for tomorrow. Are we being quiet because Lucy's napping?" Tristan asked in a whisper.

"That and because Johnny's brother is sleeping as well," Gabe answered quietly while pointing to Saint, who was asleep in the recliner.

Gabe knew something was wrong almost immediately as Vincent's face changed from curiosity to shock. "That's Johnny's brother?"

Johnny came over to the group and said, "Yeah. His name is Saint... Frank Jeffrey officially."

Tristan had turned to look at Vincent. "What's wrong?"

"That's the same man I pulled out of Venezuela four weeks back. He was among a team of doctors and nurses taken hostage while offering medical aid in-country. We were sent over to get them back. He was in rough shape when we found him. It's good to see he's recovered." Vincent turned toward Johnny, "If I had known, I swear I would have told you. I didn't know who he was other than a hostage."

"My brother was on an aid mission to another country?" Johnny looked ready to pass out. "How did I not know this? I don't know my own brother."

Gabe gathered him into his arms. "Maybe you both have been given this chance to change that."

Chapter Sixteen

Saint

He could smell food cooking, its aroma heavenly. His stomach growled in agreement. When Saint opened his eyes, he was aware of two things, he wasn't in his motel room, and the little cutie he'd operated on in Costa Rica was peeking over the edge of the chair he had been sleeping in. He wondered what the odds were that this was the child his brother had adopted, and was the same one he'd helped.

"Hello, Lucy," he whispered, not wanting to scare her. Lucy's smile was instantaneous and warmed some of the cold deep inside him.

"Saint play?" She held up two dolls and looked hopeful.

Who can say no to that? When he pushed on the chair to bring it back into an upright position, he'd momentarily forgotten about the healing wound on his stomach. The first cry brought his brother and Gabe running from the kitchen.

How can I forget about the damn hole in my side?

Johnny picked up Lucy as Gabe said, "I'm a medic with the fire department, let me have a look." Saint nodded, and Gabe raised his shirt. Shit. Saint felt weaker than he had yesterday and knew he was overtaxing himself, but things needed to be done before he headed to LA.

"Okay, it doesn't look as if you've pulled anything open, but I'd have a better idea if I knew what I'm working with," Gabe stated pointedly.

"Three gunshot wounds, stomach and both hands," Saint explained, hearing his brother's gasp in the background. "It should be okay, I have an appointment for a checkup with a Dr. Green tomorrow morning."

"How did you get shot?" Johnny asked, looking shocked.

"Some people didn't want me in their country any longer." Saint knew that oversimplified explanation wouldn't stand.

Gabe covered Saint's heavily bandaged abdomen and helped set the chair upright. The minute Gabe stepped back, Lucy decided her path was clear and insisted, "Saint play."

"Why don't you bring your dollies over to show Saint? He still has a tummy ache," Johnny suggested, and Lucy thought it over for a minute. It was amazing to see how far the little girl had come. She toddled toward the big toy box against the wall chanting, "Dolly, dolly."

When Saint looked back up, he could see the questions in Gabe's and Johnny's eyes and decided to get the rest over with as quickly as possible.

"Lucy was a patient of mine. I repaired her cleft palate and lip. She had a hard time settling down in the strange environment of the clinic so I sat with her and rocked her until she fell asleep. Over the course of the next several days she figured out my name and has been saying it ever since."

Saint waited for the questions he'd expected to come, but both Johnny and Gabe didn't say a word. Something was up.

"Saint, while you were sleeping a couple of our friends came by to drop things off for our new puppy that's arriving tomorrow. One of the men works as a Sentinel, his name is Vincent," Johnny explained, and light bulbs starting going off in Saint's head. Things kept getting stranger and stranger. Coincidence is rarely that, but in this case...

"Then you know," Saint stated, happy not to have to relive it, but wished that he'd been the one to explain.

"Not all of it. Vincent told us you were taken as a hostage in Venezuela,"

"That's where they found me. Our father had control of my professional life but he couldn't do anything about my free time. On my 'vacations' I volunteered my time with Flight for Life all over the world. I could finally put this medical training to good use, not for only increasing someone's breast size or sucking fat from their asses. I was helping people who truly needed it." Saint got lost in his thoughts for a moment, the taste of blood, the burn of bullets ripping through his flesh, the cruel laughter surrounding him...he wondered if it would ever leave him.

"Easy, Saint. You're safe, big brother." Johnny's voice broke through the haze of those dire memories, bringing Saint back to the here and now. He knew what was happening to him; he was, or used to be, a doctor and knew the signs. Post traumatic stress disorder, and he'd be damned if he'd surrender one more thing. His sanity was not up for grabs like his life's passion was.

"I'm okay. Sorting through the memories. Anyway, that's how I met Lucy and why I look the way I do," Saint explained, not wanting to delve any deeper than necessary. He noticed the key was still on the table and could use that to redirect the conversation. "That key is for you, Johnny."

Johnny turned to the coffee table and picked it up, flipping it through his fingers. "What's the key open?"

"A lock box I've brought with me. I couldn't carry it to the diner so I figured you could come back to my room and get it when you have time," Saint explained, realizing that soon he'd have his answer after years of wondering whether he did the right thing in saving it.

"What's inside the box?" Johnny asked.

"As much of Mom's jewelry as I could save."

Johnny sat with a thump onto the floor and Gabe was at his side in seconds. It would be a long time before he'd be able to move that fast again.

"You have them?" Johnny asked in disbelief.

"Well, originally Dad had them. I liberated them before he could sell them. I've been holding on to them for years, trying to figure out a way to get them to you. I know how much they meant to you, so I thought you'd like to have them." He remembered all the times Johnny could be found playing with the pieces when Mom got ready to go out.

Johnny looked at the key in his hand wistfully. Saint had wanted to give that to his brother for so long.

"Thank you, Saint," Johnny said as Lucy brought over three dolls and laid them on Saint's arm before returning to the box.

"Wait, why are you doing all this now?" Gabe asked, seemingly realizing where this conversation was going. "If it wasn't safe before, then why now?"

Saint raised his hands and looked Gabe in the eyes. "Because I'm no longer useful to him." He ground his teeth together. "I'll never be able to operate again."

"Oh, Saint. I'm so sorry," Johnny said as he stood and gave him a hug around his neck, mindful of Saint's injuries. He couldn't even remember the last time someone hugged him for no other reason but to support him. Of course, people hugged him when he'd fixed something on them or one of their relatives, but never just for him. It felt nice.

"Thank you, but lots of plans ahead. New things to learn and see." *That's it, give 'em the brave face.*

Johnny looked at him as if he wasn't buying it for a minute, but thankfully let it go. "I'm happy to have you back in our lives."

"Me too, and I'm happy you found someone who can protect you in case Dad comes calling."

"You think he will?" Gabe questioned in a voice Saint called the first responder tone.

"I hope not, but I've learned he's capable of anything," Saint answered with absolute seriousness.

Chapter Seventeen

Shadow (Jake) and Randy

Randy stood in the living room of the big old Victorian he now called home, staring at the huge, heavily decorated Christmas tree, of all things. If someone walked in on him now, they would think he'd lost his mind. Perhaps he had. Randy hadn't had a full-blown Christmas in over ten years. His parents decided to skip the "hoopla" long ago in favor of sunny vacations in tropical locations without him or Grady. After Grady had moved out, Randy had spent the holidays alone.

He wasn't sure how he should feel about the change. Overwhelmed was the first emotion that came to mind. This Christmas he'd be celebrating with a town and house full of people, and for some reason that had him unsettled. Randy had never belonged to anything. It wasn't that he didn't want to have his new friends around him during the holidays, quite the opposite. He even had a healthy relationship with his brother, Grady, again. But it had been a long time since Randy had trusted anyone, and even longer since strangers became friends. He imagined he'd be able to handle what was coming because he had Jake. The strong, kind, courageous man he loved. Randy had a lot to be thankful for this year. He hoped he could handle it without making a fool of himself.

For a long time now, all he'd wanted was a normal family, especially around the holidays, and he was frustrated that doubt and trepidation clung to him like the tinsel on the tree. Everything was perfect and he still wasn't settled. He huffed and ran the palm of his hand down his face before he turned and walked to the kitchen where Mrs. Walker was busy baking Christmas cookies. He couldn't remember a time he'd ever seen his own mother baking anything, let alone cookies. Randy had to admit he'd never eaten so well in his life. Mrs. Walker was a cooking goddess.

"Hi, Mrs. Walker," Randy murmured. His voice sounded flat and he knew it.

"Well, hello there, Randy," she replied before giving him a shrewd look. "Why don't you come over here and help me for a bit. I could use another pair of hands."

Jake was busy in town, and everyone else was off working on personal projects. Randy had thought he might finish a painting he was working on, but helping Mrs. Walker seemed a better distraction. All he was doing was making himself feel worse, so why not help out. "Sure. But I warn you, I've never baked cookies. This could turn out badly."

"No worries, hon. You sit right there and I'll get you an apron." *Apron?*

Randy took his seat at the large kitchen island and waited for Mrs. Walker to return. The room smelled like a bakery, and the counters were covered in flour, cookie cutters, bins, bowls, icing, and candy. After a quick look around, he helped himself to a mini candy cane. He was a sucker for these little buggers. He used to buy a bag of them and stash it away in his dresser to have throughout the year.

He popped it into his mouth as Mrs. Walker came back into the kitchen with a bright red and green reindeer apron decorated with "XMAS" in big white letters across the front. The nose of the reindeer sparkled with red glitter, proclaiming him as the one and only Rudolf.

"Here you go, young man," she said as she handed the apron over. "I'll get a bowl set up for you to mix."

She looked so delighted with the ridiculous apron that Randy put it on. Jake had explained about the White Hair Crew, and somehow Randy wasn't surprised that in a town like Brighton there was a gang of do-gooding grandmas. As he'd explored his new hometown on his daily bike rides, people would wave at him and say hello. One day when the chain fell off the temporary bike he was using, so many vehicles stopped to help that they created a mini traffic jam on the normally quite country road.

Mrs. Walker placed a bowl full of dry ingredients and one that had wet and fluffy ingredients in front of him. She handed over a big wooden spoon and instructed, "Now you need to add the dry mix slowly to the wet until it's blended."

Randy looked at both bowls with the spoon in this hand. "Are you sure I can't mess this up?" He imagined the guys biting into a cookie and spitting it out in disgust.

"I trust you will do fine." Mrs. Walker smiled. "Now get to it. We've got lots of people to feed."

He couldn't help but smile back and got to work. Over the next several hours they mixed, rolled, cut out various Christmas shapes, baked, and then decorated, once the cookies were cooled. As time went by, and with Mrs. Walker's commentary and knowledge, he began to feel a certain calm settle over him. As members of the household dropped in for a cookie or three, they praised Mrs. Walker and him on their cookie-making skills.

His fingers were stained red from icing, he had flour on his face and in his hair, and his fancy apron was covered with a little bit of everything, but he felt happy. Slowly, Randy allowed himself to feel connected to the people and rhythm of the house as they joked, ate cookies, and downed hot chocolate like it was going to disappear.

Randy was laughing along with everyone else when he noticed the man of his dreams hanging back and watching him with a smile on his face. Jake stood leaning against the back wall, arms crossed, biceps bulging. Randy wasn't sure how long Jake had been standing there watching him, but he had the need for a little Jake time.

His lover crooked his finger. It seemed as if Jake needed a little Randy time as well. He wiped his hands on the dishtowel lying on the counter, picked up a Santa cookie, and joined Jake, who now stood with his arms open wide.

Randy looked down at the front of himself. "I'm a mess."

"Don't care," Jake said before pulling him close. "Having fun, babe?"

"Believe it or not, this is the first time I've ever baked cookies," Randy said proudly as he presented Jake with his Santa.

Jake brushed flour off Randy's cheek and forehead. "You look like you're an old pro at it."

Randy knew Jake was teasing him and loved him all the more for it. Jake took a bite of his cookie and his eyes went wide. "This is really good."

"Don't look so surprised. Mrs. Walker taught me. I'm thinking of trying my hand at baking every so often."

"I'm all for it. I love Christmas," Coop cheered before stuffing his mouth with another candy cane cookie.

***

Shadow led his talented boyfriend back to their suite of rooms that was much the same setup as the other guys' rooms. He had a large bedroom, en suite, and a lounge space with a television and couch. He could hear Bits, Randy's puppy, trailing behind them. The two of them had a special bond. Bits was the runt of the litter, and was so small, but he was a fighter just like Shadow's Randy.

They'd been able to move all of Randy's artwork, at least the ones he'd managed to save after his father destroyed so many beautiful pieces, to the room next door because it had the best light, according to his partner. It was set up as his studio for now until they decided if they were going to build a home of their own. Shadow wasn't in any hurry to undertake a big project quite yet; he wanted to enjoy the gift he'd been given and let Randy become acclimated to their lives.

It had been only three and a half months since he'd found this special man chained to a wall, and it had been crazy busy ever since. Between protecting Randy while he healed, and getting his life back together with everything from identification to underwear, the poor guy hadn't had a chance to slow down and ease into the new and different world Shadow had brought him into

Shadow had noticed the lost, unsure look in his lover's eyes on several occasions, and he hoped to address that right now. He opened their bedroom door and Randy bent to scoop up Bits before smiling at him and walking in. His gasp was instantaneous, and Shadow was unsure if that was good or bad. He shut the door behind them and followed Randy to the center of their suite.

"Jake, it's...beautiful." Randy's voice was filled with awe.

Shadow looked around at the hideaway he'd created for Randy with the help of his friends. While his man had been busy baking cookies, a few of the guys hung out in the kitchen to keep him distracted while the rest were in here. Their plain king-size bed had been replaced with a stylish, rosewood four-poster bed. The dark, reddish brown wood complemented the thick, dark red drapes that flowed from around the bed and covered the windows. He'd enlisted his mom as well as the team and their partners to make sure he got it right. Shadow was the first to admit he didn't know a thing about decorating or romance.

Battery-operated candles that were incredibly real-looking glowed around the room without the fear of causing a fire. After all, they had a puppy. Thick plush pillows and a blanket covered their bed, and potted poinsettias dotted the room. In the lounge area, two stockings hung above the gas fireplace, and a smaller, personal Christmas tree stood proudly in the corner with presents already wrapped stuffed underneath it. The room was decked out to be warm, cozy, and Christmassy. Exactly as Shadow had planned. All that was left was to explain.

Randy set Bits down so their puppy could explore. Shadow took his partner's hand before leading him to the Christmas tree. "I know that everything is strange and different for you. You haven't really had a chance to relax and take it all in."

"I'm okay, Jake," Randy said with a smile, but Shadow knew his man was trying to keep him from worrying. The one thing Shadow had learned about his boyfriend, Randy always thought of others first.

"You're more than okay, you're fantastic, but this hasn't been easy on you. So, I've made us our very own hideaway. The mini fridge and cabinet are stocked, microwave and Tassimo stand at the ready, and whatever we don't have we can sneak into the kitchen and liberate." Shadow took Randy into his arms and held him tight. "We're going to slow down now, me and you. I've even downloaded a lengthy list of Christmas movies for us to watch while we cuddle by the fire. Christmas Eve after the wedding ceremony, we'll stay for dinner, wish them our best, and sneak away back to our hideaway. Christmas morning, we'll open up our presents in here, only the two of us, before joining the rest of the team. I don't want you to feel rushed or uncomfortable."

Randy's eyes were still wide but he had a big smile on his face, so Shadow took that as a good sign. Until the tears started. After the first drop fell, he quickly gathered Randy into his arms and sat down on the couch. Shadow wasn't sure what was wrong, but he had to fix it.

"I can take it all down if you want me to."

"Don't you dare, it's perfect," Randy muttered as he sniffled. "How did you know this is what I needed when I didn't even know?"

Shadow could feel the weight of worry being lifted from his shoulders. Randy wasn't upset, he was happy. He looked up at Shadow with those warm amber eyes and Shadow could read every emotion: relief, happiness, surprise, all went flittering across Randy's handsome face, but most importantly, love.

"Because I know how hard you try to make other people happy without any thought for yourself. The mural that took you weeks to complete, the decorations, always smiling and meeting all the new people who live and work in Brighton, and then helping around here in between working on your art and baking cookies. You haven't slowed down since getting free of that hellhole. So, from now until after the New Year, we're hiding out in here. We'll go out when and if we want, and for no other reason. Oh, except to take out Bits to do his business, but then that's it."

Randy wrapped his arms around Shadow's neck and hugged him tight. "It's perfect. Thank you, Jake."

"Your welcome, sweetheart," Shadow replied before realizing he'd forgotten one of his surprises. "I've got something for you for Christmas, but I'd like to give it to you now, okay?"

"Jake, you've already given me so much."

"You'll need this, and it's for your safety."

That got Randy's attention. "I think I'm the safest I've ever been in my entire life already."

"You'll understand when you see it." Shadow stood, leaving Randy to wait on the couch.

He went to their en suite and opened the door. It only took him a couple moments before he called out, "Close your eyes." His lover complied and Shadow wheeled out his surprise in front of the Christmas tree. "Okay, open them."

"Jake…" Randy stood and joined him in front of the tree. "It's… I don't want to keep saying perfect, but it's the only word that fits." Randy ran his fingertips over the frame of his new bike. Shadow knew how much his man liked to go biking even though he couldn't go long distances because of his weak lungs. This bike was one of the lightest Shadow could find, and it was made by hand and guaranteed to not leave Randy stranded anywhere.

"This one won't leave you stuck on the side of the road, like that other one did."

Randy picked it up and said, "It's so light. How much did this cost you?"

"You can't know or argue because it's a Christmas present," Shadow stated matter-of-factly.

"Christmas present, huh?"

"Yep, those are the Christmas rules, honey. I didn't make them, but I'm not going to piss off the big, bearded guy by breaking them." Randy laughed as Shadow had hoped. "Want to try it on for size?"

Instead of throwing his leg over the bike as Shadow had expected, Randy put the kickstand down and said, "I can think of something else I'd prefer to do."

"Yeah, and what's that?" Shadow asked as he rounded the bike and pulled Randy into his arms.

"I think I need to get all this flour off me with a soak in a deep bubble bath. Would you be interested in joining me?" Randy asked as he kissed the side of Shadow's neck, making his body perk right up.

"Oh yeah, you bet your cute ass I do. Go start the water and I'll pour us two glasses of wine."

Randy's eyes were truly windows to his soul, and Shadow could see his future in their depths. With one final kiss, Randy turned and walked into the en suite. Shadow couldn't look away until the door shut, his man was that mesmerizing.

Finally, he forced himself to the fridge, pulled out a bottle of Chardonnay, and uncorked it. Shadow looked around his personal space, for years it had been empty and soulless. Suddenly, colors were flooding his world again, bringing back emotions he'd thought all but lost. His room was like a mirror to his soul, now filled with life and light. All thanks to the amazing man waiting for him in a tub full of hot, soapy water.

Shadow reached out and grabbed two wine glasses along with the bottle. He had some new memories to make.

Chapter Eighteen

Rick, Bear, and Josh

Five days before the wedding

Bear looked out at the heavily decorated dining room from the kitchen's serving window. Rick had outdone himself. He swept the booths and counter, confirming the dinner crowd had finally slowed enough for him to go over the new stock that had been delivered earlier in the day.

"Hey, Jesse. I'm headed to the back to check out the order."

"I got it covered, boss man," Jesse replied, making Bear grin. The guy was more family than employee, but he still called Bear boss man. Bear would miss having Jesse around after Haven opened, but understood that running the center would take his full attention and time. Of course, the diner had hired more cooks, and between Jesse and Travis's training they were ready for the changeover, but Bear would miss seeing his friend daily.

He left Jesse in charge and walked to the back of the diner and the storeroom. He flicked on the single light hanging by its cord in the middle of the room and grabbed his clipboard from the top of one of several skids of product. There was triple the amount of food in this order to account for Johnny and Gabe's wedding. He still had to go through the freezers and fridges after this. It was a huge undertaking, but he'd prepared for that. The diner would be closed Christmas Eve day and Christmas day so that he and the White Hair Crew could do final preparations.

Johnny had asked for the food to be set up buffet style so that people could go for more food any time they wanted. There were quite a few big men who lived in town who'd be in attendance and they could pack away a ton of food. It would be like serving almost everything on the menu all at once, as well as a few new dishes Rick had convinced him to serve. His lover was always his biggest supporter, and especially Rick loved it when Bear was working on new recipes. With all the planning done, he'd been prepping for days. The entire twelfth grade would be working at the event to ensure everyone had lots to eat and drink during the course of the evening. It was a good way for them to earn some volunteer hours.

Bear was roughly halfway down his list when he felt a pair of warm hands sliding around his waist. Bear knew those hands. He looked down at the ring he'd put on that finger sparkle in the light. Everything was right with the world once again.

"Hey, babe, come for a visit?" Bear asked as he turned around to face Rick, his lover and partner in everything. He took Rick's lips in a deep kiss that had him completely forgetting about stock, orders, and the countless preparations that needed to be done. Instead, his body was acutely aware of the handsome man in his arms.

When he finally let Rick up for air, he answered, "Yep, I came to visit. You've been working so much lately with Christmas and the wedding coming up that we haven't had much alone time." Rick tried for his best pout, and Bear had to admit, his man was adorable. "Josh is with the gang of grandmas, and Jessie is in the kitchen. We have a solid fifteen minutes, baby, let's not waste them."

Bear chuckled as he closed the stockroom door and placed a heavy box in front of it so that no one could walk in on them. He remembered when they first met, Rick was the quiet librarian. He was still that in some ways, but sex wasn't one of them. Rick knew what he wanted and wasn't afraid to ask for it.

"There isn't enough time for me to prepare you properly and I refuse to hurt you no matter how much we want each other," Bear explained as he rubbed his hands down Rick's back on his way to squeezing his ass. He liked to take his time and make sure Rick was ready and comfortable.

"I've already taken care of that, Bear," Rick said while wiggling that cute ass of his.

"You're not teasing me, are you?" Bear reached down and unzipped his lover's pants before pushing them to the floor and off Rick's socked feet. Bear took only a moment to wonder where Rick's shoes were before he reached around and found what he was looking for. "A butt plug, you smart, horny, sexy man. Thank God."

Bear didn't think he had the patience left to wait now that he knew his lover was ready. Rick had been telling the truth, Bear had been working long hours lately and they hadn't made love in over a week. That changed today. Bear flipped Rick around and braced him against a skid full of bagged linens wrapped in packing plastic. He licked and sucked his way down his lover's neck, making Rick moan and push his ass out invitingly.

He couldn't resist playing with the butt plug and aiming for Rick's prostate, when his love went off, he knew he'd found it. Over and over again, he pulled the plug out before sliding it back into his lover's ass, taking him a bit higher with every move. Rick used his own arm to muffle his moans in an attempt at not alerting anyone to what they were doing.

Bear reached for one of the stacks of clean linens and pulled out a couple of towels, placing one on the floor. He'd gladly pay for a few missing towels. Rick's body was shaking in Bear's arms as he removed the plug and set it on the towel, then he handed the other one to Rick for better muffling. Quickly, Bear undid his jeans, hissing when he pulled his boxers over his hard cock. He blanketed Rick, and with one more kiss he pushed deep inside Rick's hot, tight ass.

They both groaned out their pleasure when Bear's balls touched Rick's cheeks. Every time the two of them made love, Bear lost himself to the feel of his fiancé's body. His soft skin begged to be touched and worshiped. With his arms wrapped tight around Rick, he lifted him off the floor to get the right angle in order to send his lover even further into a world of sensations and pleasure.

Rick arched his back, allowing Bear to go a touch deeper and driving him on even faster. His hips pistoned back and forth as the sounds of flesh slapping and moans of pleasure filled the room. Bear mastered Rick's body, exactly as his lover liked it, leaving nothing untouched.

Moments later he felt Rick stiffen before his body clamped down on Bear's cock. Spasms rocked through his man and into Bear, pulling his orgasm from his body without warning. He buried his face in Rick's soft hair and groaned as he came deep inside his lover.

Bear held on to Rick's limp body as they both recovered in a haze of gasping breaths and aftershocks. Their stolen moment was slowly coming to an end and he was loath to release Rick quite yet.

"Love you, Bear," Rick murmured as he rubbed the side of his face against Bear's chest.

"Love you so much, Rick," Bear replied while letting out a deep breath. "We are never waiting that long again. I swear."

"Hallelujah."

Chapter Nineteen

Dante, Spider, and Sam

The emergency room was unusually quite that morning and it gave Sam the time he needed to catch up on the never-ending pile of work growing wild on in his computer. He loved being a nurse and helping people, but could do with a touch less processing work. He was in the back office surrounded by Christmas cookies when he looked up through one of the interior windows and saw Johnny and a man, who had to be his brother, approaching the admissions desk. The family, hell, most of Brighton had heard of Johnny's brother already, and a few knew what he'd been through.

Sam stood up, walked out of the office, and approached them as they were checking in with the admissions clerk. "Hello, Johnny."

Johnny looked up and smiled. The guy was one of the happiest men Sam had ever met. "Hi, Sam." Then he pointed to the other man. "This is my brother, Frank Jeffrey, but he goes by Saint. He has an appointment with Dr. Green," Johnny said and went on to explain to his brother, "Sam is one of Gabe's cousins."

Sam could see the bandages and noted the exhaustion in Saint's eyes. "Nice to meet you. How are you feeling today?" *Awful, by the looks of you.*

"Holding strong," Saint stated before taking his information back from the clerk. "Thank you for all you did for my brother."

"No thanks needed, we're family," Sam assured, but he saw Saint cringe at the word "family." He also looked like he was ready to fall over. "Why don't you guys follow me and I'll get you settled in a room."

On his tablet, Sam looked up Saint's file, and then led them to a quiet room in the back to give them as much privacy as possible for an ER. Sam chose a space without a window so that the big man could rest without the daylight bothering him.

"You didn't have to come with me, little brother. I'm capable of bringing myself where I need to go. I don't want to take you away from all your wedding plans so close to the event," Saint grumbled as they entered the patient assessment room.

"You're my brother and you look like you're ready to pass out. There's no way in hell I'm leaving you to your own devices. I love you, and I don't want to see anything else happening to you," Johnny argued, which had Saint smirking.

"What happened to the kid who couldn't stand up for himself?" Saint asked.

"He grew up and had a family. Now, lay your ass down on that gurney and rest until the doctor gets here," Johnny ordered. Sam couldn't help but smile. Johnny was the sweetest guy you'd ever want to meet, but when it came to the health of someone he loved, he was a pit bull. Okay, maybe not a pit bull, maybe a French bulldog, but those pipsqueaks could take you down with the right motivation.

Saint lay down on the gurney without another complaint. Well, he certainly grumbled but didn't say a word. Sam took Saint's blood pressure and temperature, both were a bit high, and he noted everything in the exam screen on Saint's chart. With gunshot wounds, medical staff had to watch out for any possible infections, and an increased temperature could be a sign that Saint was fighting one. Sam wrapped rubber tubing around Saint's arm so he could draw blood, but the band wouldn't stay on. The man's bicep was huge.

"I'll have to get a longer one of these, be right back." Sam left the room and went to search the shelves of medical supplies in the back room. He found what he was looking for, pulled out a longer piece of tubing from the roll, and cut it.

When he walked back into the room, Saint was nearly asleep but Sam needed him awake for the blood draw. "Saint, you need to stay awake for me while I take your blood."

His eyes popped open so fast that Sam doubted Saint realized he was falling asleep. Johnny had been quiet since he'd gotten his brother onto the bed, watching everything going on. Once Sam had finished drawing two vials, he placed a small gauze square over the small hole the needle had made, then wrapped mesh adhesive over the gauze.

"I'll take these to the lab and alert Dr. Green that you're here, Dr. Jeffrey," Sam told Saint as he gathered up his tablet and the vials of blood.

"Not doctor. Call me Saint," he responded before laying his head back down.

Sam looked over at Johnny, who seemed heartbroken, before saying, "Okay, Saint it is." On his way out, he squeezed Johnny's shoulder. This had to be difficult for both of them. Sam put a rush on the blood work and headed to Dr. Green's office.

The doctor's door was closed so Sam knocked and waited. It didn't take long for Dr. Green to answer. "Hey, Sam, what do you have?"

"Frank Jeffrey is in exam room ten for his appointment. I've noted his blood pressure and temperature are both high and took his blood to be tested and have a CBC and panel done up."

"How does he present?" the doctor asked.

"He appears to be exhausted and in pain. I won't be surprised if he's sleeping by the time we go back in. Also, don't call him doctor, he doesn't like that." Sam didn't want to upset the man a second time by using the word.

"Okay, the blood work will give us a better insight into whether he's fighting an infection. Go grab the supplies to clean and redress his wounds while I go introduce myself."

"On it." Sam returned to the back room and gathered everything they might need: sterile instruments, dressings and tape, along with sterile saline to clean the wounds. He stopped by the meds room and prepared a syringe of pain reliever in case it became necessary. By the time he returned to the room, Dr. Green was waking Saint and introducing himself. It seemed that the patient was having a hard time waking up. When he finally did, Saint looked confused.

"Mr. Jeffrey, how are you feeling?" Dr. Green asked.

"Tired, but I'll fix that with a couple hours' rest." Saint's voice was gruff before he cleared his throat.

Dr. Green listened to Saint's heart and lungs before lifting his shirt and examining the dressings. "We'll get these changed for you, Mr. Jeffrey, and have a look at how you're healing."

"Saint, please. They call me Saint."

"Okay, Saint. Sam, will you start with the left hand while I begin with the stomach wound," Dr. Green stated. "Have you taken you pain medication today?"

"I try not to use them."

Dr. Green picked up the syringe from the tray. "I'm afraid this will be far too painful without some sort of pain medication."

Saint agreed with a nod. He was giving the shot before Sam would begin removing the bandages from his left hand. Sam would have hated trying to clean these wounds with the man feeling one hundred percent of the pain. Sam never liked causing anyone pain, although it was inevitable in his profession. He and the doc donned their gloves and went to work.

Johnny stood by the head of the bed and laid his hand on Saint's bicep while Sam revealed more and more damage with each layer of removed gauze. Saint never flinched. Not when the gauze stuck to one of his sutures or when Sam cleaned the pitted wound running through the center of his heavily sutured hand.

Dr. Green cleaned and bandaged the wound on Saint's stomach and was moving on to his right hand, and still not a peep out of their patient. Sam had to look up on several occasions to make sure Saint was okay, but the man was staring at the ceiling. The only indication of pain came from the beads of sweat on his forehead. Sam tried to be quick but careful to make sure the wound was thoroughly cleaned and healing.

Care and precision meant it took a while before they finished, but the wounds were completely cleaned and bandaged. By now Johnny was the one who looked like he was ready to pass out, and Saint was drifting back to sleep. The exhaustion and medication finally caught up with the poor guy.

Dr. Green stepped to the rolling computer outside of Saint's room to check the status of his blood work. Sam came around the table and took Johnny into his arms. "He'll be okay, he's healing. I promise."

"What kind of person would do that to another human being?" Johnny's voice cracked as he spoke, his emotions getting the best of him.

"Animals, plain and simple. No one with a conscience could do that." Sam could feel the anger coming off his friend. "Don't waste your energy on anger. There is nothing you can do to change it. Your brother needs you to be strong for him."

Johnny seemed to consider what Sam had said as Saint began to snore, loudly. Dr. Green came back in the room with a concerned expression on his face.

"I see our patient is asleep but he did sign the release to discuss his healthcare with you, Johnny. Do you want to sit down?" Dr. Green asked.

Johnny stood tall and squared his shoulders. "I'm fine, thank you. Can you tell me if my brother is going to be okay?"

"The wounds are severe, as you saw, but they are healing. He is fighting a small infection and to be on the safe side I'd like to hook him up to some fluids and antibiotics. He needs to remain in the hospital for a couple days until he's stronger. I don't feel comfortable releasing him given the shape he's in currently." Dr. Green looked Johnny straight in the eyes. "Can you convince him of that? I had a look at the original hospital records and found he'd checked himself out against doctor's orders after his last surgery to repair the damage."

Johnny's eyes opened wide. "He didn't mention anything about that. Don't you worry, Dr. Green, he'll be staying right here until you feel it's safe for him to leave." Johnny crossed his arms and looked down at the sleeping man with conviction and affection.

Sam couldn't imagine what Johnny or Saint were going through. Being apart for so many years only to come together under the stress of everything that had caused these severe health concerns. There was nothing Sam could do to change what happened, and listening to his own advice, he stood strong.

Sam wrapped his arms around Johnny and said, "I'll be right by your side, buddy."

Chapter Twenty

Jesse and Royce

Jesse wandered through Haven in the early hours of December twenty-third. In the predawn light, he walked the halls of this place where his dreams had come to life. He couldn't stop the goose bumps from rising when the oranges and yellows danced across the walls from the sunrise peeking over the trees. He ran his hand across the solid walls as he passed, strong walls to protect all who would come here.

He knew that soon enough these halls and rooms would be filled with people from all over connected by a single thread of hope. Hope that this time, in this place, they'd find what they were looking for and the help they needed.

The trained staff he'd hired would ensure that the people were safe and cared for, giving each of them the one thing they'd been denied: a chance. Everyone needed a chance to build a future for themselves, to learn, and to grow without fear and pain, and then to go on to help others. Yes, this was his dream, and he'd do anything to see it succeed.

Jesse sat in one of the new desks at the back of one of the many classrooms. This would be where Mrs. Connor would teach English. More rooms down the halls were set aside for science and math, as well as rooms that would be devoted to budgeting, taught by a retired CPA, and the ever-important cooking, and how to do laundry taught by the White Hair Crew. These young people would be coming here lacking basic and complex knowledge and skills that Jesse wanted to provide for them so they were able to learn how to cope with the world, and have the choice to move on to higher education, if they so desired.

He understood that the core classes were essential, and they wanted to assist those who were missing their GED to get it. The life classes would change and grow as needs were discovered. They were working with Shannon from the Sentinels to teach a self-defense course, and an art class led by Travis. There was also a chance for horticulture, which had been thrown into the ring by Sam, first aid led by Royce, and creative writing led by Tristan. Many others in the town wanted to help. Even a few ranchers had offered to teach whoever was interested how to work on a farm, and with animals.

Things were coming along better than Jesse could have ever imagined, and he recognized that without the townspeople's help, none of this would have ever happened. Brighton had accepted and protected him. It had given him his first real home and a way to support himself. It brought him Royce, a gift that had changed his life and filled his heart.

Jesse headed back to the main offices, passing the pool, first aid station, computer room, and cafeteria. The front of the building had sweeping, wide steps to welcome people in, and a wall of glass adorned the front of Haven. Once inside, comfortable couches and chairs were dotted every few feet, making sure everyone had room to study, chat, or sprawl. The front desk was well lit and cheerful. People standing at the desk waiting for assistance would be able to see Randy's inspiring artwork on the far wall.

The storage rooms were filled with clothing, shoes, toiletries, and school supplies. The cupboards, fridges, and freezers were full of nutritious food and drinks. The whole building was standing at the ready for the day they opened at the beginning of the New Year. Jesse had been fielding calls from schools and other shelters as word of Haven spread.

The sun rose above the trees, bathing the front of Haven and Jesse in its warm glow. He walked over to the metal plaque he'd had commissioned from one of the local artisans. As he ran his fingers over the letters and words, one thought remained centered in his mind. His grandpa would have been proud.

Welcome to Safe HAVEN
To All the Souls that Enter, May You Find
Peace and Safety Here.
Dedicated to the Town and People of Brighton, Texas
And in the Loving Memory of Grandpa Roy Tribalt

As a single tear rolled down Jesse's cheek, he could hear his grandpa and what he'd written in his will for Jesse to read.

Believe me when I say you will find a love that will fill all the empty places in your heart just like your grandma did for me. Be a smart man, and hold on to it as hard as you can because if anyone deserves to be happy it's you.

And Jesse was truly happy.

Chapter Twenty-One

Gabe and Johnny

The heavenly sound of steak sizzling on the barbeque filled the backyard of Gabe's best friend's house. Gabe could hear his stomach growling at the thought of a thick, juicy steak. It was the evening before his and Johnny's wedding, and they were having a barbeque at their best men's house. Royce was standing up for Gabe and Jesse was doing the same for Johnny.

Gabe was positive their family and friends were knee deep in bows by now, and busy decorating Haven for the wedding and reception. Johnny and Gabe had been warned to stay away under pain of a tongue lashing from the White Hair Crew. Taking the admonition seriously, the four of them were having a quiet night before tomorrow's ceremony and festivities. Johnny had settled down now that his brother was out of the hospital and resting comfortably in the spare bedroom at their house.

Thankfully, most of the wedding preparations had either been completed or assigned, so they had this night to relax. They'd picked up their suits today, the last thing on their list, and had chosen not to be separated before the wedding. Traditions were made to be broken, and there was no way they would be apart. And in keeping with doing things their way, they'd decided to walk down the aisle together.

Lucy was already asleep in Royce's spare bedroom, having had her dinner before everybody else. Of course, the trusty baby monitor was never too far away, in case she needed them. Gabe pulled his soon-to-be husband closer as the two of them cuddled under a blanket on the deck swing. Their friends had set up outdoor heaters so that the area would be comfortable, which helped, but they still would be eating inside.

Jesse was manning the grill as Royce handed out another round of beers and asked, "So any nerves, you two?"

Gabe was quick to answer. "Not a one." He couldn't wait to make Johnny his husband.

Johnny, on the other hand, had a different take on the upcoming nuptials. "Of course."

"What do you have nerves about, babe?" Gabe asked out of curiosity. Maybe he could help.

Johnny was quick to look up at him. "Not about marrying you, that's the best part of tomorrow. Everything else is what's worrying me. What if there's a problem with the food, or the flowers? What if we don't have enough chairs or tables, or if there's a freak snowstorm?"

Freak snowstorm. Gabe nearly laughed, but knew his man was stuck in worst-case scenario mode, worrying everything wouldn't be perfect.

He reached out and cupped his fiancé's face in his hands, humbled by the love and trust in those brilliant green eyes. "Babe, as long as you become my husband, the day will be a success. The rest can work itself out. It's time to relax and enjoy this moment together." He took Johnny's lips in a deep kiss, expressing his emotions through his touch.

Every word was the absolute truth, and them getting married was what mattered. As far as Gabe was concerned, the rest was for everyone else.

From the moment Johnny had come into Gabe's life, he knew he'd been blessed. The quiet, unassuming man, who'd saved two lives in the fire that brought them together, was a gift. The love they had for each other was so strong that they'd decided they needed to share it, and now they had their daughter. There had been a time when Gabe had pretty much given up on his own happily-ever-after. Now he had his soon-to-be husband and a beautiful daughter, his family to love and care for.

Gabe had everything he'd ever dreamt of, and it was all due to the man in his arms.

Chapter Twenty-Two

December 24th – Wedding Day

Johnny was losing his mind and no one seemed to care. Okay, maybe a bit overdramatic, but his kitchen was flooded. The dishwasher had decided today of all days would be the perfect day to have a crisis mid-cycle. Every towel they owned lay covering the kitchen tile in an attempt to soak up the soapy water.

Saint stood looking from the safety of the dining room with Lucy in his arms as their new puppy came around the corner and slid through the bubbles. Gabe had left in search of some sort of part they needed to fix the traitorous machine, and Johnny stood front and center of his own nightmare. Today was supposed to be calm and joyous, not soggy and soapy.

"Chill, bro, it'll be fine. The wedding is still hours away. I've got Lucy. You don't need to worry about her. She'll be ready to go." Johnny knew his brother was trying to calm him, "trying" being the operative word. The good news, Saint looked much better now that he'd spent a few extra days under medical care, relieving some of Johnny's worry.

"You're hurt, you need to be resting and recuperating, not chasing a toddler around." Johnny wanted to crawl back into bed and start over. He knew he was already strung tight, but this wasn't helping, and now his brother risked his recovery to help him. Not going to happen.

"No worries, a young woman named Josie called to say she'd come help me today. She said she's Gabe's cousin. Is that the one you told me about in the fire, the one you grabbed onto outside the window?"

"Yep, that's Josie. She called you? How did she get your phone number?" The home phone hadn't rung.

Saint squinted before he began to grin. "I don't know. I didn't even think about it. Could this be one of those Brighton things you told me about?"

Johnny couldn't help but smile. "That would be it. Once the town's people decide you're family they swoop right in."

"Not entirely a bad thing, little brother," Saint observed, and Johnny understood the draw that kind of life had to each of them. Even before their mother had died, life was less than ideal for them under their father's rule.

Johnny heard a truck pull in and assumed it was Gabe back from the store, until there was a knock on the front door. He dried his wet feet and went to answer it. When he opened the door, he was confused as to why Mr. Tucker, from down the street, was standing there with a Santa hat on and his toolbox in his hand.

"Hello, Mr. Tucker. How can I help you?"

"You've got that the wrong way around, young man. It's what we can do to help you. We heard you had a bit of an issue this morning and we've come to help," he told Johnny while holding up the toolbox.

"We've?" Johnny looked behind the older man to find his wife and Mrs. Walker, from across the street, carrying mops and pails. "I can't ask you to do that."

"Who asked?" he inquired before walking in and headed to the kitchen followed by his smiling wife.

"Don't you worry, we'll get things to right in no time. You go sit down and rest. You have a big day ahead of you," Mrs. Walker ordered before following the first two "helpers" into the other room.

Johnny stood there staring at her retreating figure, unsure what just happened. Saint came over with a strange look on his face, but said nothing.

Johnny looked at his big brother and said, "Yep, it's a Brighton thing."

***

Hours later Johnny was doing his final tour of Haven, taking in that all the decorations were up, the flowers were delivered, and seats were all set for the ceremony. In a nearby room, tables had been pushed together against the far wall, and covered in lovely tablecloths to hold the buffet dinner. After that the room would become their dance hall.

Everything looked even better than he had imagined. The decorations, in rainbow shades, were spectacular. Ribbons and bows hung around the room and on the chairs, while small twinkling lights shined in various spots along the walls. They intended to have the overhead lights muted during the ceremony, giving the room a more intimate feel.

A twelve-foot, fully decorated Christmas tree glowed from the front of the room where they'd be exchanging their vows, with Father John officiating. Poinsettias bloomed from hand-decorated pots, and orchids stood tall in their elegant beauty. Johnny had insisted on having orchids from Gabe's greenhouse at the ceremony. His love had labored over them especially for today. His mom would have loved that.

"How you doing, sweetheart?" Gabe asked as he came up behind Johnny and hugged him to his broad chest. Johnny couldn't help but melt into Gabe's arms.

"It's all so beautiful," Johnny's voice cracked as he spoke. "I'm overwhelmed that so many people came together to give us this. I just..." He wasn't sure what was happening. He felt like he was having an emotional breakdown.

Gabe spun Johnny around and gathered him in his arms. Johnny couldn't help but reach for the comfort his love was offering. Everything was so real, and yet he felt he was drowning at the same time. He needed a minute to come up for air. Gabe reached down and picked him up, then carried him out of the room.

He heard a door shut and looked up to see where Gabe had taken him. They were in their assigned consultation office/change room. A desk and chairs were set up to the right while an orange couch stood against the back wall. The bathroom door was open revealing a mirror, sink, and toilet. The sparkle from the rubies and emeralds of his mother's vintage brooch, pinned to the lapel of his suit jacket, caught his eye.

"Why did you bring me here?" Johnny asked.

Gabe sat down on the couch before rearranging Johnny, turning and lying down with him on top of Gabe's chest. "Because this is where you and I are going to hide out until the ceremony."

"But there's so much to do." Johnny's mind was racing. "What about Lucy?"

"Lucy is completely happy with her Uncle Saint and Cousin Josie. As for everything else, there are a lot of family and friends out there to take care of it. Right now, all I want is to be alone with you before you become my husband." Gabe kissed Johnny's forehead.

Johnny got comfortable on Gabe's chest and concentrated on his lover's strong heartbeat. Gentle fingers began running through his hair, helping him settle even further.

"When we first met, I knew you were special. The one person just for me," Gabe murmured, his voice vibrating through his chest as he spoke. "The person who would teach me how to trust again and open my heart to a future. Never having to live with doubt or fear again. Without you, Johnny Jeffrey, I am nothing."

"I thought you were crazy," Johnny deadpanned, making Gabe laugh, as he'd hoped. "However, after the initial shock wore off, I realized I'd found my home and my family. At first, I worried that you were too perfect and my dreams would be taken away from me at any moment, but we stood strong together. You helped me gain back my independence and a career I love. You're my anchor, my love, and my life. Without you, Gabe Mason, I am nothing."

They spent a few moments holding each other in silence, the air thick with emotion. "Why do I feel like we just exchanged our vows," Gabe teased as he snuggled Johnny closer. "We couldn't have said it any better."

***

Later that evening the two lovers walked hand in hand down the aisle with their special flower girl at their side. They made their heartfelt vows before their family and friends, new and old, in the small town of Brighton, Texas.

What began in the flames of a fire was now completed in the glow of holiday lights. The community gathered to share their love and joy with the happy new family in the season that embodied the mandate of peace, love, and joy. Laughter and songs could be heard late into the evening and early the next morning.

Thank you from everyone in the town of Brighton for joining us as we watched the trials and tribulations on the road to love between people who deserved a happily-ever-after.

The Gates of Heaven series begins.
We're in DTLA (Downtown Los Angeles) where we'll follow Saint as he attempts to start over.

EXCLUSIVE EXCERPT

SAINT

Book One in the Gates of Heaven series

Saint stood at ground zero among the tattered fabric from the sweeping drapes clinging to twelve-foot-tall windows long boarded over since the heyday of this building. Walls covered in bubbling, flowered wallpaper, and furniture left broken and forgotten lay haphazardly among the rolled-up rugs, which had fallen over from where they'd probably been lined up against the walls. A single shard of light pierced the dust-speckled air as if it was a beacon leading him onward in this incredibly misguided undertaking.

A sweeping staircase stood dead center in the vast space. Its worn and broken railings seemed to smile with gaping holes, laughing at him and the insanity of it all. Chandeliers hung in a macabre fusion of spider webs and layers of dust. Crumbling plaster left walls open, and piles of debris could be found everywhere he looked on the dirty marble floors.

On the far wall stood a large fireplace that suspiciously resembled an open maw ready to gobble him whole. The furniture in the long-ago lounge area stood strangely at the ready with its Hollywood Regency style still evident in the faded tufted velvet chaise awaiting some former movie star's arrival. He could swear the original plaster moldings above the doors, windows, and bordering the ceiling were inspired by Dorothy Draper herself.

"So that's everything." The real estate agent beside him spoke and he nearly jumped, having half forgotten she was standing there. She winged up a painted brow then handed him the keys. "Good luck, Mr. Jeffrey." Then she was gone, moving quickly through the thick wooden double doors, scurrying to induce some other idiot sucker into investing in a broken-down wreck.

Saint walked across the lobby to the incredibly intricate front desk covered in brass and what appeared to be deep, rich cherry wood. He set his bag down on its worn surface and caught his reflection in the cracked sunburst mirror behind the desk.

Tired blue eyes stared back at him as he asked himself the all-important question of the day.

"What now?"

ABOUT THE AUTHOR

M. Tasia lives in a small town in Ontario, Canada. She's a member of the Romance Writers of America and its Rainbow Romance Writers and Toronto Romance Writers chapters. Michelle is a dedicated people-watcher, lover of romance novels, '80s rock, and happy endings. Also, she's the mother of two wonderful girls, wife to a great husband, and servant to two spoiled furry children who don't seem to realize that they're actually cats.

Michelle writes contemporary and paranormal romance, and she believes love should be celebrated. After all, everybody needs a little romance, excitement, intrigue and passion in their lives.

Connect with Michelle:
mtasiabooks.com
facebook.com/mtasiabooks
twitter.com/mtasiaauthor
instagram.com/m.tasia.author/

Did you enjoy this book? Drop us a line and say so. We love to hear from readers, and so do our authors. To connect, visit www.boroughspublishinggroup.com online, send comments directly to info@boroughspublishinggroup.com. Friend us on Facebook and follow us on Twitter and Instagram. And be sure to sign up for our newsletter for surprises and new releases in your favorite subgenres of romance.

Are you an aspiring writer? Check out www.boroughspublishinggroup.com/submit and see if we can help you make your dreams come true.

Made in the USA
San Bernardino, CA
30 January 2019